A LOVE SO TRUE

A GREATEST GENERATION LOVE STORY

CAROLINE MICKELSON

BON ACCORD PRESS

*Dedicated to the memory of
my grandmother,
Rose*

～

*A young war-bride
from England, she had
a heart of gold and
was truly the kindest person
I've ever known.*

CHAPTER 1

a magnificent bomber's moon shone over the city of London, illuminating it as a perfect target for German planes hell bent on destruction. It would be hours before the sun would rise and free the city's inhabitants from yet another tense night of air raid sirens and incessant bombing.

Emma Bradley silently thanked fate for the bright moonlight as she hurried across Cumberland Road. Like her fellow Londoners, she'd learned to find security in the nighttime darkness that offered protection from enemy aircraft. Tonight, however, she was fleeing the city she loved and the man she hated. The moonlight was a gift.

The sound of raucous, slurred singing reached Emma's ears only seconds before three soldiers turned the corner and headed toward her. Fighting a raising panic, she tightened her hold on the baby in her arms. She glanced around quickly, looking for a doorway or a place to hide.

There was nowhere safe.

As the soldiers grew closer, and Emma could see they were more drunk and far rowdier than she'd first thought, a wave of fear washed over her. She squared her shoulders and drew the blanket over the baby's face. "Everything will be fine, little one," she whispered to the sleeping newborn. She'd make sure of it.

Only a few hours earlier Emma had carefully selected a few items to take out of London with her, knowing full well the most she could manage to carry would be the baby and one valise. The rest of her possessions she'd given away to neighbors or left in her rented flat for the landlord to sort out. What she'd given up, she didn't care about. It was what she stood to lose that mattered.

She looked up at the three men who now blocked her way.

The soldier closest to her gave a low whistle. "What's this? A lovely lady looking for an escort home?"

Emma moved to pass the man, but he reached out and grabbed her. "We aren't going to hurt you, lady. What's the matter with you?" He pulled her closer to him. The smell of ale on his breath was over-whelming. "We just want to spend a little time with you."

"Let me pass," Emma commanded. She wrenched her arm free of his grip. She'd give them just the one warning. No one, certainly not a few drunken soldiers, would get anywhere near the baby. Not while she drew breath.

The man reached out to grab her again as the other two men closed in. Emma backed up, instinctively pulling the baby to her chest.

"I'll scream bloody murder if you don't get away from me this instant." Emma heard the fear in her voice as she spoke. She took a deep breath. Now was the time to be brave, to sound strong. "You're drunk, the lot of you. Go on your way."

"Shut up," the taller soldier snapped. His eyes settled on the bundle in her arms. "What's this then? What are you trying to hide?"

He reached out a hand to touch the baby but Emma slapped it away.

"You little bitch--"

His tirade was cut off by a low growl emitting from a dark shadow behind him.

Emma's cry of surprise caught in her throat. The two other soldiers slowly backed away, their eyes wide. As desperate as she was to keep the soldier from touching her baby, she could only pray that this enormous shadow of a man wasn't a worse threat than the soldier before her.

In an instant, swiftly and silently, the man in shadows grabbed ahold of the soldier in front of her and slammed him up against the building. "I'm going to let you go so that you can apologize to the lady."

Emma stared, transfixed, as her rescuer abruptly released his hold. The soldier stumbled before finding his feet. He took a deep shuddering gasp of air. The bright moonlight illuminates his frightened features. "I'm sorry, so sorry, ma'am," he stammered. "I meant no harm."

"Get out of here. Now."

The soldiers needed no more prompting than that. They took off running without a backwards glance to see if she would be safe with the man who so clearly terrified them. When they were out of sight, she turned back to the stranger.

But he wasn't beside her. "Wait a moment, Sir, please," she called to his retreating back.

He continued walking as if he hadn't heard her.

Emma hesitated. She needed to thank him. God only knew what he had just saved her from. But she hesitated. What if he had been sent by Malcolm?

But that made no sense. If Malcolm had sent the man, then why had he come to her defense? And why would he walk away if he had been sent to bring her back? Her fear was making her delusional.

Was she going to live this way forever? Were Malcolm's threats going to wield control over her, leaving her always fearful? Emma looked down at the baby and caressed his sweet soft cheek.

Malcolm could rot.

"Wait, please," she called to the stranger's retreating back. "Please allow me to thank you for what you did for me."

The man stopped walking and turned to face her. "Do you need assistance returning home?" he asked.

He had an accent. Somehow that surprised her. It shouldn't though. Since the war started all manner of foreigners were about.

But she couldn't quite place it. He wasn't American, nor did he sound German.

"I'm not going home." She walked toward him. "I've a train to catch at Paddington in two hours." Emma couldn't make out his face in the shadows yet her fear abated as she drew closer.

"Perhaps it is safer if I were to walk with you?" His voice was low and cautious but far less gruff than the tone he'd used with the soldiers only moments before.

Emma hesitated. Surely walking the darkened streets of London with this man couldn't be any more dangerous than walking alone?

She glanced around. The streets were deserted. The skies were quiet. She knew that air raid wardens were on duty throughout the city but would they hear her if she called for help? Probably not.

The man held out his hand and nodded towards her valise.

She handed it to him. Doing so left her better able to hold the baby, which was what truly mattered, that she keep the baby safe and away from Malcolm.

"Thank you," Emma said as she shifted the baby from her left shoulder to the crook of her right arm. He was still asleep, which she considered a blessing. She prayed it was a sign of a smooth journey to their new home.

The man began walking and Emma fell in step beside him. He was far taller than she was, and his stride so much longer than hers, that she struggled to keep up. She was reluctant to ask him to slow down though. He'd done enough to help her for one night.

The sound of Emma's heels on the sidewalk filled the space between them. The man beside her didn't seem inclined to talk. Her arms grew numb from holding the baby, but her heart lightened with each step she took. For days she'd expected something to go wrong, waited for some obstacle to present itself that would prevent her from leaving London. But, finally, she dared to hope that she and the baby were on their way to safety.

The wail of an air raid siren shattered the quiet of the night, startling the baby into a frightened cry. Emma silently cursed the Luftwaffe. Why now? She glanced up into the darkened sky. How far were the incoming planes from the city?

Her companion turned to her. "You need to find a shelter." He looked around. "Are you familiar with this part of the city?"

"No. I mean, yes, I am," Emma had to raise her voice to be heard over the siren. If she joined the people filtering out of their homes and into the air raid station, heaven only knew when the all clear would sound. It could be hours, time she couldn't spare. "I'm not going into a shelter."

His frown was swift and ferocious. "You need to take the baby to a safe place."

"That's exactly what I'm doing." Emma ignored his words and reached out a hand for her valise. "I thank you for your help earlier but I need to catch my train. I can't stay here." Not if she wanted the baby to be safe.

"Foolish."

Despite the siren's warning wail, she heard him clearly enough. Surprised, she glanced up. This time the moonlight favored her with a clear view of his face.

His jaw was strong and square. His nose was long and straight, and his hair was a shade of blonde. He radiated a quiet strength. But it was his eyes that captivated her. They were light colored, blue or green, she couldn't be sure in the moonlight, but they were arresting. Emma could see wary uncertainty in the way he looked at her.

An elderly woman bumped Emma's elbow as she passed by, startling the baby into an angry cry. Emma closed her eyes against the madness of the moment. The baby's cries, the siren's incessant wails, the laughter of small children heading towards the shelter, the adults attempting to quiet them; it all juxtaposed into a surreal insanity.

Emma longed to be free of the noise, the crowds, the threat of falling bombs, and the overwhelming, constant sense of impending doom. Nazi aircraft had dropped bombs for seventeen straight nights and who knew when the bombardment would end? Was she meant to wait days, weeks, or even months for there to be a quiet night so she could travel? No. Waiting was out of the question. There was a safe place near the seaside waiting for her and the baby. All she had to do was get there.

She looked up into the man's eyes again. He hadn't taken his gaze from her, and it left her feeling suddenly self-conscious. She shook her head. There was no time to debate this. "I'm going on to the train station. You don't need to understand. No one does."

Instead of answering, he put a hand under her elbow and guided her through the throngs of people heading into the underground station. She breathed a sigh of relief when she realized he wasn't guiding her toward the shelter, but away from it. To her surprise, Emma found she didn't fear his touch. Heaven only knew who he was, but for tonight she'd consider him a guardian angel if he helped her get to the train station on time.

They continued along the way, passing dozens of people in various states of dress, most staggering half-asleep on their way to a shelter. Many women were carrying a baby or were shepherding several small children.

How frightening must it be to care for children in a city under siege? She thanked heaven she wouldn't have to find out. She'd been initially resistant to the idea of leaving London, adamantly refusing to give the Nazis the satisfaction of driving her out of her home. But she had more than herself to think about now.

If she stayed, the first sounds her baby would hear in life would be that of shattering glass, enemy aircraft overhead, and ambulance sirens. His tiny lungs would fill with smoke from the bombs that dropped around them.

But most worrisome of all, was knowing she'd constantly be looking over her shoulder for fear that Malcolm would find them.

THE WOMAN HAD TO BE MAD. SHEER LUNACY ALONE WOULD EXPLAIN why she was walking unaccompanied through the streets of London in the middle of the night. He glanced sideways at her. Hardly alone, was she? She held a tiny babe in her arms, which only made it harder to understand why she was not seeking shelter in the underground like any other reasonable woman would.

Not that he was an expert on reasonable women. Or any other sort of woman for that matter. Before the war he lived the life of an internationally renowned concert pianist. From Paris to Madrid, Toronto to Buenos Aires, he had been surrounded by beautiful women wherever he performed. But spending time with a woman, and understanding her, were two different things altogether.

He glanced sideways. Next to her he felt tall but it was she, in truth, who was quite petite. Petite and lovely. He hoped that she hadn't been able to read his expression when he'd looked at her. She was enchanting, the picture of loveliness. Her husband was a fortunate man indeed.

Andrej was grateful not to have to think of what to say because she lobbed questions at him, one after the other, but he kept his answers as short as possible. His reticence, however, did nothing to silence her because she began to share her opinions of each and every member of the new Prime Minister Churchill's cabinet. Was she always this talkative or was her chatter a result of her nervous state?

What didn't escape his notice was that she spoke not a single word about herself. Her refusal to seek shelter told him that she was both determined and single minded. And desperate. Why else would she be walking through the darkened streets, alone except for the baby in her arms?

"What did you think about the Under Secretary's decision?"

Andrej stopped walking and looked down at her. "What is your name?"

"Emma," she said after a moment's hesitation. She began to walk and he fell back in step with her.

Emma. It suited her, he thought.

Fortune was with them as they made their way through the darkened streets. They didn't encounter a single air raid warden, which allowed them to continue on without anyone questioning why they were out so late.

Andrej's thoughts turned to the news he'd received the day before.

After months of looking for suitable employment that would accept a non-British passport holder, he'd finally secured a position in Brighton for the duration of the war. He knew little about the work he was to do except that his ability to read and write several Slavic and Scandinavian languages had secured him the job.

Truthfully, he didn't care what manner of work it was. He just wanted to be a part of the war effort in some way. His passport was Dutch but his life involved so much travel that he didn't consider himself a true citizen of any one country. The outbreak of war in Europe had curtailed his nomadic lifestyle. Wealthy patrons of his had encouraged him to come to America to wait out the war in New York but he'd been strangely reluctant to leave Europe. The response of His Majesty's subjects throughout Britain had inspired him to be a part of something more than his music. Finally, here was his chance to be someone other than a gifted, celebrated musician who, at the end of the day, belonged nowhere and with no one.

All that he had to do was get to the train station, see this lovely but stubborn woman safely on her way, and then catch the train that would take him to the seaside and his new life.

"I hear planes," Emma's voice interrupted his thoughts.

Andrej stopped and strained to listen. She was right. The sounds of their engines were faint but they were growing louder. He glanced around their surroundings and noticed a flight of steps that appeared to lead down to a basement flat. There were only eight or so steps but some protection was better than none.

"Come this way." He placed a hand on Emma's back and guided her toward the stairwell. Once they were at the bottom of the steps he set her valise down and motioned for her to have a seat on the bottom step.

The baby began to fuss and Andrej watched as Emma shifted the now wiggling bundle from one shoulder to the other. She cooed and made soothing sounds but the baby continued to cry.

Andrej searched for something reassuring to say as Emma's earlier bravado had clearly faded away. He had no experience with children. In fact, he did everything he could to avoid them. He couldn't even remember the last time he had actually seen a baby, he knew for certain that he'd never held one.

Avoiding children was how he avoided painful memories. Yet here he now was, standing in a tiny stairwell with a woman and child. As he watched Emma's attempts to soothe the baby he couldn't help but wonder if his mother had ever done the same for him. An all too familiar coldness spread through him. "You should have gone to the shelter," he said.

Emma looked up at him. "The all clear sounded."

"Judging by what we hear, I'd say that was a tad premature, wouldn't you?" He listened for the sound of aircraft. Although he heard it, it was impossible to judge how far away the planes were without knowing how many of them there were.

"If something happens to me tonight I need you to promise me something," Emma said.

Andrej looked down at her and felt an unfamiliar tightness in his chest. He could hear the fear in her voice. "You will be fine."

"You don't know that." Emma moved to his side. "If I'm hurt I need you to take my baby--"

"This isn't the time to grow hysterical," he interrupted her, his words sharper than he intended.

She clutched his arm. "You don't understand. I'm all my baby has. If I'm not here, take the baby out of London. Wales perhaps, anywhere you find an orphanage."

He stared at her, shaken by her rising panic. "Tell me where your family lives."

She shook her head resolutely. "There's no one. The baby and I are alone in the world." Her eyes filled with tears but her voice remained tight and controlled. "You need to take him as far away as possible. Promise me."

Silence wasn't the answer she needed. He knew he ought to tell Emma to control herself, to calm down, but instead he nodded his agreement.

Emma took a deep steadying breath. "Thank you."

A rush of tenderness such as he had never felt before washed over

Andrej as he looked down at her hand resting on his coat sleeve. He wanted to reassure her but he didn't trust his voice not to betray him. What was it about this woman that she affected him so?

The drone of aircraft engines grew closer. Only a fool wouldn't grasp the serious threat of planes as close as these were. "Go sit on the bottom step, hold the baby close to you," Andrej instructed her. He shrugged out of his overcoat and place it over her in the hopes it would protect her and the baby from shattering glass. He settled on the step above them, positioning his body as best he could to shelter her.

The only thing left to do was brace for an explosion.

They didn't have to wait long before the low whisting sound warned the bomb was on it's downward path to destruction. The ensuing thunderous blast was immediately followed by the sound of shattering glass and then far-off ambulance sirens. From where they were hunkered down, Andrej was unable to see anything. But the fact he couldn't smell smoke meant that the bomb had dropped a relatively safe distance away.

Andrej lowered his coat. "You and the baby are safe, Emma." He slipped a steadying arm under her elbow and helped her to her feet.

She turned her face up to him. Her eyes searched his. "Thank you," she said, her voice barely above a whisper.

Andrej didn't know what possessed him but he reached out and tucked a strand of her hair that had come loose back into place. When she didn't flinch at his touch, his chest tightened and he drew in a deep breath. "Come. Let us get you to the rail station." Once they were back on the sidewalk, he scooped up her valise with his right hand and offered her his other arm. She smiled gratefully as she slipped her arm through his.

As they walked in silence, Andrej realized that just this once, just for tonight, he hadn't been hurt by taking a chance on caring for someone other than himself. Even if it was a woman he would momentarily say goodbye to and never see again.

CHAPTER 2

*E*mma pulled the edges of the crocheted blanket closer around Patrick's little body, snuggling him inside her half-buttoned jacket in an attempt to keep him warm. She loved the feel of his tiny heartbeat so close to hers.

The chilly September wind cut through the crowded train station. Lacking the warmth of the sun, the dawn was no warmer than the night had been.

She scanned the passengers milling about before she checked her watch again. Ten more minutes and the train would pull away from London and take them toward the safety she so craved. If, of course, her traveling companions were on time. She bit her lip. Where were they?

Her eyes continued to search the platform for a sign of them.

She did a double take when she glimpsed the man from last night. He stood at the opposite end of the platform under a light reading a newspaper. Only his profile was visible but she was certain that it was him. His height and the breadth of his shoulders set him apart.

Was he waiting for the same train she was? Emma frowned. Last night she watched him leave the station. When saying goodbye, they'd faced each other for a long moment before, ever so quietly, he'd whispered, "Goodbye, Emma." His eyes held a kindness that she hadn't been shown in such a long time, and she'd become so overwhelmed with emotion that she'd barely been able to offer her thanks before he walked away.

But what was he doing here now? She didn't even know his name. She considered again the notion that he could be working for Malcolm but just as quickly she thrust the thought aside. The people Malcolm surrounded himself with were a coarse, uncaring, blood thirsty lot. This man had treated her with great kindness. No, the idea they were somehow related was ludicrous.

The respectful way she'd been treated the night before seemed a heaven sent reminder that there was such a thing as a man who wasn't cruel, violent or hateful. She needed to remember that, especially if she were going to raise little Patrick to be totally unlike his twisted father.

"The six-thirty morning train for Brighton is now available for boarding at platform eight," a rail attendant called out as he walked the length of the platform. The noise in the station swelled as passengers said their good-byes.

Emma stomped her feet to try to keep some feeling in them. The cold she could manage to keep at bay, her fear wasn't so easily banished. What on earth was she meant to do if they didn't arrive?

"Emma?"

She spun around, hugely relieved to hear a familiar voice. "Thank goodness you're here. I was starting to worry." Emma's smile faded as she took in the other woman's tear-stained face and swollen eyes. "Oh, heavens, Laura, I'm so sorry."

Laura nodded. "I didn't mean to give you a fright about being late, but it's just been so hard to face sending the children away," her voice broke on the last two words.

Emma glanced down at the two young children standing beside their mother. Seven-year-old Peter kept his eyes downcast. His older sister, Lily, stood stoically on the other side of her mother. Emma smiled as reassuringly at the little girl as she could. Lily didn't smile back.

The platform was rapidly emptying. An elderly porter bustled toward them, a sympathetic expression on his lined face.

Laura nodded. "I know. It's time now." She bent down and gathered her son and daughter into her arms. "This won't be forever my little loves. The moment it's safe for you to come home, I'll send for you straight away." She stood and looked both children in the eyes. "You must promise to be brave and strong until it's time to come home."

Peter nodded but didn't speak. He gazed from his mother to Emma, confusion playing across his face.

"Mummy, you mustn't worry about us," Lily said in a voice that was doubtless meant to be reassuring, but sounded young and vulnerable to Emma's ears. "We won't be any trouble. You'll come to visit us though, won't you?"

"I'll try, love. I promise, but you know the hospitals are full and all the nurses are needed here in the city." She smoothed her daughter's hair affectionately. "If I can get any weekend leave I'll come down to visit."

Laura grabbed Lily and held her tight. Peter threw himself at his mother and sister, and they embraced him.

The touching sight tore at Emma's heart. "I'll protect them with my life, Laura."

"Ladies," the porter interrupted them apologetically. "I'm sorry to hurry you along but it's time to board now." He took up Emma's valise and the two small satchels that they'd brought with them. "Come along, children."

Laura kissed each child quickly and motioned for them to follow the porter. "Go on then, loves, it's time to start your adventure. Mummy will write to you, I promise."

The two women watched as they followed the porter up the steps and onto the train. Laura waved goodbye until the children were out of sight. She then turned to Emma, tears streaming down her cheeks.

"I've given Lily an envelope for you with information about the children that might be helpful." Laura looked at her pleadingly. "You'll write to me, won't you?"

Emma swallowed the lump in her throat and nodded. "Yes, of course, Laura. I'll let you know how they're getting on." She glanced over her shoulder to the porter who was beckoning her.

There was so much she wanted to say to her friend, so much reassurance she wanted to offer, and promises she wanted to make, but words failed her. She reached out for Laura's hand and squeezed it reassuringly. After a quick hug, she hurried toward the train. The porter pulled the steps up behind her and gave a signal to the platform manager.

Emma made her way to where Peter and Lily sat waiting for her. She settled in the seat across from them. Finally being off her feet felt heavenly, knowing she was only moments from leaving the city was blissfully reassuring, but watching the children with their little faces pressed against the glass waving goodbye to their mother, was painful.

As soon as the station was out of sight, both children sat back in their seats and looked expectantly at Emma. What could she possibly say to ease the heartache so clearly etched on their little faces?

The enormity of what she'd taken on when she'd agreed to watch them suddenly hit her. She'd only met the children once before. Laura worked with Emma's cousin Patricia in a surgery quite close to the Whitehall office where Emma worked, and the three women often shared tea breaks. Until, that was, Patricia's funeral several weeks earlier, when Emma had confided in Laura of her plans to take Patrick, her cousin's baby, and find work outside of the city.

Three days later Laura had come to Emma with a proposition. If Emma would agree to take her two children out of the city, Laura's brother-in-law would use his connections to obtain Emma a position with a guaranteed billet for herself and the three children.

The offer had seemed heaven sent. When they'd met at Hyde Park for an afternoon out, the children had struck Emma as well mannered and easygoing. Now, sitting across from them, their intent little eyes upon her, Emma wasn't so sure if she was up to the challenge. But after her cousin's death, Emma hadn't thought herself up to raising Patrick alone either, had she? Yet here she was. Here they all were, and there was nothing for it but to forge ahead.

"We'll do our best to be happy until it's time to come home," she finally managed to say. "I think the best way to pass the time is to try to be as busy as possible each day until your Mummy and Daddy come for you."

"Daddy's missing," Peter said in a near expressionless voice. His gaze never left Emma's face.

Her heart sank. Oh, these poor children. Poor Laura. Emma struggled to keep her face composed because Lily and Peter were both watching her closely.

Was this what it meant to be a mother? Keeping one's own emotions carefully in check so that your child would be comforted and reassured by your every word?

"Mummy just received word last week that Daddy's been reported as missing in action. We don't know more than that, but Mummy says we mustn't give up hope," Lily said, her voice quite matter-of-fact. She looked at Emma with a seriousness that belied her small porcelain face and long brown braids. "I heard Mummy tell Gran it's likely an error of some sort. And then Gran told Mummy that if anyone could mix-up important information, it would be the French."

"Oh, Lily, I'm so sorry to hear this." Emma laid Patrick down on the empty seat beside her in the makeshift nest she'd made for him with her coat before she turned back to the children. "I agree with your Mum and Granny that it could well be an error. We'll have to wait and pray every day until the war is over and your father returns home."

Lily nodded. "You sound like Mum."

"Do mothers always know what to say?" Peter asked. He looked over at Patrick. "Oh, you haven't been a Mum long at all have you, Mrs. Bradley?"

Emma winced at the unfamiliar moniker, but she needed to get used to it. Now that she had Patrick with her, people would quite naturally ask questions about the non-existent Mr. Bradley. "Would you find it agreeable to call me Aunt Emma, perhaps?"

When both children nodded, Emma was relieved. Maybe this wouldn't be as difficult as she'd first thought.

"We can help with the baby," Lily offered. "Mind you, I doubt Peter will be of much use. However, I'm sure there's plenty I can do to help."

Peter frowned at his sister before he turned to Emma. "I can so help. I can do anything Lily can." He paused and wrinkled his nose. "Except for nappy changes, of course."

Emma laughed. "I will handle all of the nappies, you needn't worry. However, I do need some water for Patrick's bottle. Do you think you could find a steward and ask them for hot water?"

Peter shot a triumphant glance in his sister's direction. He reached out for the glass bottle Emma offered, nodding his understanding that he mustn't drop it. After Emma gave him instructions, he headed confidently in the direction of the beverage car.

"Do you think he'll be all right?" she asked Lily.

"Peter's always fine," Lily said in a tone that was equal parts annoyance and pride.

ANDREJ ACCEPTED A CUP OF TEA FROM THE STEWARD WITH A GRATEFUL nod. Most of his thirty-eight years had been spent living around the globe. However, since the outbreak of war in Europe, he'd lived exclusively in Britain. Somewhere during that time he'd gone from considering a cup of tea a quaint local custom to a daily necessity.

He took a slow sip and savored the strength of the brew. Granted, he'd have liked it laced with cream and sweetened with sugar but this was war time after all. Such luxuries would have to wait until Hitler was defeated.

Andrej glanced over his shoulder as two women walked through the beverage car, but he knew without looking that Emma wasn't one of them. One wore far too much perfume and the other laughed too loudly. A desire to see her again tugged at him but he knew he was safer staying where he was. In a short few hours together the evening before, Emma had made a powerful impression on him, unlike any woman before ever had.

Something troubled him though. Earlier, when he settled into his seat, he'd glanced out the train window and had seen Emma speaking with another woman. A woman she obviously knew well from the way she was appearing to comfort her. Hadn't Emma said she and her baby were all alone in the world?

He shook his head as if to dismiss Emma from his thoughts. He wasn't going to see her again, and undoubtedly this was for the best.

A school age boy stepped up to the beverage counter. He lifted a baby bottle and set it on the counter, then hoisted himself into the seat adjacent to Andrej's. The boy looked around for a steward, and when he failed to find one, he turned expectantly to Andrej.

"Good day, Sir."

Andrej suddenly wished the drink in his hand was a good deal stiffer than tea. Children unnerved him. This one, judging by his confident air and the way he looked Andrej straight in the eye, might well prove to be especially unsettling.

"Hello." Perhaps if he said as little as possible the boy would wander back from where he came.

"Have you seen a steward about?"

Andrej took another sip of tea before answering. "He's just stepped away but I imagine he'll return shortly."

Silence. That wasn't what he expected. Andrej looked over and met the boy's stare. He lifted an eyebrow in question.

The boy swallowed hard but didn't look away. "Are you traveling home, Sir?"

"No."

"So, you live in London then?"

Andrej shook his head. Where was the blasted steward anyway?

"Interesting," the boy said solemnly. "My name is Peter. That's an English name." He waited several moments before he spoke again. "Is your name English?"

Andrej set his tea cup down and turned to face the boy. "No. It's not." What on earth else was there to say? He couldn't remember the last time he'd sat and conversed with a child, but he found it far more taxing than conversing with an adult. "Did you need something?"

"Yes, of course, I'm meant to fill this with hot water but I don't see the steward." He leaned forward in his seat and propped his elbows on the counter. "I daresay it's best to just wait here." He looked expectantly at Andrej.

So it was his turn now. Perhaps he was safest just turning the lad's questions back on him.

"Are you traveling home, Peter?"

The little boy shook his head. Fair turn about, Andrej thought. What question had the boy countered with? Ah, yes. "So you live in London then?"

Peter seemed to need to think about that one.

"You don't know if you live in London?" Andrej prompted.

"I did until this morning," Peter answered gravely. "My Mum still does. She's sent my sister and me to live in Brighton until the bombing stops." He sat straight up in his chair and a hopeful look crossed his face. "Say, do you know when the blitz will stop?"

"No, Peter, no one knows when, or even if, it will ever be over," Andrej said, and then immediately regretted his choice of words. Peter looked as if all his hopes had been dashed. Confound it. He was going to throttle that cursed steward if he ever came back.

Peter slid off the seat and took the baby bottle down from the counter. "Do you know something about Germany's plans?"

"No, of course not," Andrej hastened to say.

Peter nodded. "I see."

Just what the child thought he saw, Andrej didn't understand. He felt like an idiot as he watched the boy depart. Relieved, yes, he was that too. However he hadn't meant to suggest the war would never be over. He frowned. How literally did children take things?

An old and all too familiar sadness threatened to return from the recesses of his memory. Damnation. Andrej rubbed his temples. This was precisely the reason he avoided children. They brought back memories of loneliness, of confusion, and the slender thread of hope he'd desperately clung to for years that his mother would return for him. The frightened little boy he'd been had grown into a man who had learned that he could live quite contentedly, so long as he avoided prolonged contact with people.

Peter, though, was just a child. The least he could do was fetch the water the boy needed and get it to him, along with an apology of course, and a reassurance that the war couldn't possibly last much longer. Andrej stood, pushed his now empty tea cup away, and looked around. Where was that excuse for a steward?

~

"I swear he was a real Jerry," Peter insisted to a disbelieving Lily and a confused Emma. "I sat right next to him, and he as much as assured me the war would never end."

Emma had gone limp with relief when Peter returned. He'd been gone so long that she'd just begun to worry when he had reappeared with a delighted twinkle in his eye. And not a drop of water in the baby's bottle. She wanted to press him for an explanation about the water but Lily was already grilling her brother.

"I'm to believe that you sat next to a Nazi spy?" Lily questioned him. "Oh, really, Peter. This is outside of enough. Next you'll tell us that you met Princess Margaret Rose in the corridor. Oh, and wait, don't look over your shoulder but isn't that King George behind us?" She threw in a dramatic sigh and a roll of her eyes to let her brother know exactly what she thought of his tale.

Emma opened her mouth to ask about the water but Peter rushed to his own defense.

"Don't be a silly girl. My questions were clever enough that he didn't even know he was being questioned." Peter puffed out his chest. "I got him to confess that he doesn't live in London yet he says he's not journeying home either."

"That's it?" Lily demanded.

"No, that is not it. I also got him to admit that his name is not English." Peter cast a triumphant glance at both women.

Emma held her hand up quickly, lest she never get a turn to speak. "What about the water for Patrick's bottle, Peter?"

"Oh, yes," Peter said. "I waited for the steward but he never came back."

"Right then, you two stay here and I'll go in search of water."
Emma stood and gathered Patrick up in her arms. He wasn't a fussy
baby by nature, but hunger could turn the sweetest of kittens into the
fiercest of lions. "You both stay right here and behave yourselves
properly." She couldn't resist teasing Peter, "And no more espionage
while I'm gone either."

Emma was grateful for the chance to stretch her legs. She had to
admit that she was delighted with Lily and Peter, but she was also
becoming increasingly aware of how much time and attention they
were going to need. They spoke as if they were little adults, but they
were still so young and vulnerable. She only hoped that the school in
Brighton was still open so that they could be around other children.

Who was this person that Peter had spoken with? She probably
shouldn't have sent him off by himself. She'd have to watch him more
closely if he had a penchant for interviewing strangers.

Was being a good mother instinctual? She hoped not. Although she
hadn't given birth to Patrick, she loved him already more than her
own life. She'd happily devote the rest of her life to raising him into a
fine, upstanding man his mother would have been proud of. Perhaps
she'd develop maternal instincts as she went along, but all she knew
for certain was that she had to keep him away from his murdering
bastard of a father.

What she really wanted was reassurance that she was doing the
right thing. Even the smallest heaven-sent sign would fortify her
resolve.

The train car began to lurch sharply just as she reached the
vestibule door. A small cry of surprise escaped her lips as she tightened her hold on the baby. She staggered backward a few steps, her
left hand reaching for something to steady herself.

"I've got you." An arm encircled her waist and drew her back
against something solid. "You're safe."

Emma's smile was one of relief. She knew that voice. It belonged
to her sign.

CHAPTER 3

"Thank you," Emma said as he released his hold on her. She turned around and smiled warmly.

He didn't return her smile. His expression mirrored his concern. "Are you alright?"

She nodded. "Perfectly." Blue. His eyes were an incredible shade of blue. The moonlight had made it difficult to tell their exact color the night before, but here in the daylight she saw that they were the color of the sky on the finest day of summer. "How lovely to see you again," she said, meaning the words. There was something reassuring about his presence, whether due to his imposing size or his quiet manner, she didn't know.

He nodded but didn't move aside. His eyes were locked on hers.

She found it hard to look away. "I'm sure this is a sign I'm meant to learn your name."

"Andrej."

"French?" she asked.

He shook his head with a wry smile. "Dutch." His eyes traveled to the empty bottle she was carrying. "You're in search of hot water?"

"Yes," Emma nodded. "How did you know?" Perhaps he had children of his own. She realized she knew nothing about him.

"I met Peter while he was on his quest for water." Andrej held up a still steaming teapot in his right hand. "Is he your nephew?"

"No. Peter and his sister are my wards until it's quieter in London." She looked down at Patrick, who was sucking on his tightly curled fist with all of his might. Poor hungry babe, she needed to get him fed. She glanced at the teapot and then up at Andrej. "Would you be good enough to carry the water to our seats?"

"Of course," Andrej answered. "I would like a word with Peter anyway."

Emma raised a questioning eyebrow. "What has he done?" She had rather hoped that Peter had kept his Nazi theory to himself. Wait, Peter hadn't mistaken Andrej for a German, had he? Surely not.

"It's more what I've done, or said, actually," Andrej answered as they made their way through two cars. "I might have implied that the war was never going to end."

"Well, that's how it feels often enough, isn't it?" Emma said over her shoulder. "I'm certain that Peter is fine. However, join us, won't you?"

She was relieved to see that the children were sitting quietly waiting for her return. The look on Peter's face when he saw his Nazi behind Emma was priceless though. She could barely keep the grin off of her face.

"Andrej, I'd like you to meet my young charges, Peter and Lily." She paused as Lily politely offered a greeting. Peter waved a sheepish hello but remained uncharacteristically quiet. "This is Mr--" Emma realized that she hadn't yet learned Andrej's surname. She looked up at him apologetically but he saved her from having to ask.

"Andrej Van der Hoosen," he nodded to the children. "A pleasure to meet you, Lily. Nice to see you again, Peter."

Emma sat across from Lily and motioned for Andrej to sit beside her. Lily held Patrick while Emma pulled out a small packet wrapped in brown paper. She had precious little of the homemade formula left so she was especially careful not to waste even a tiny bit as she mixed it with the water.

Conceding to Lily's pleas that she be allowed to feed Patrick,

Emma handed the bottle to her and watched as he began devouring its contents.

Emma turned to thank Andrej for the water but stopped when she saw the intent way he was looking at the baby. The sadness on his face was palpable, it was as if a cloud had covered the sun. Was he thinking of his own children, perhaps? If so, she felt for him. The war was cruel the way it separated families meant to be together.

She glanced next at Peter. "Peter, Mr. Van der Hoosen mentioned that you two had spoken of the war."

Andrej tore his gaze from the baby to look at the boy. "I spoke out of turn, Peter, when I said the war might not end. Of course, you know that it will be over one day."

Peter nodded confidently. "Oh, yes, I know that. Mummy told me so."

Emma glanced sideways at Andrej to see what he thought of Peter's answer.

"You believe everything your mother tells you?" Andrej asked in a voice so low that Emma had to strain to hear his words.

"Yes, of course, I do. My mum only tells us things as they are. Straight up, isn't that right, Lily?" When his sister nodded, Peter appeared pleased that she'd so easily agreed with him. "Wasn't your mum the same way?"

A long silent moment passed before Andrej shook his head. "I don't remember, truthfully." He rose from his seat to stand in the aisle.

Emma looked up at him. "Must you leave so soon?" Emma asked. "We've plenty of scones and enough hot water left to make tea."

Andrej shook his head. "Thank you but I cannot join you." His gaze lingered on the baby for a long moment before he spoke again. "It was a pleasure to meet you, Lily. Peter, enjoy the remainder of your journey."

When he looked at her he took his time before speaking. Despite the chatter of other passengers, and the eyes of both children upon them, Emma felt as if she and Andrej were as alone as they had been last night on the deserted city streets.

"I wish you a safe journey, Emma." And then he was gone.

∼

Not even the threat of Nazi invasion could keep British Rail from maintaining its punctual schedule. Emma peered out of the window as the train slowed. She looked up and down the length of the platform for a sign bearing the station name but saw none.

She beckoned to the porter standing a few rows ahead at the front of the train car.

"Yes, Ma'am?" he came to stand beside her seat. He glanced down at the children and a smile touched his face. "Would you be requiring assistance with your baggage?"

"I'm not even certain this is the right station." She handed him a slip of paper with the name of the place she'd been told to disembark at. "Would this be where we alight?"

Emma watched as the porter's eyes scanned the paper without saying anything. She shifted in her seat. She was tired, beyond sleepy, and felt grubby and in need of a wash. And nervous, definitely nervous. The last thing she needed to do was disembark at the wrong station.

"Not returning home then, are you?"

"We're relocating," she answered. Then realization dawned. She remembered reading in *The Times* that British Rail had removed station signs to confuse possible German spies. Understandable definitely, but certainly inconvenient. But then nothing about wartime was convenient.

The porter smiled kindly. "It's a sad day in His Majesty's Kingdom when I can't tell a young lady such as yourself where you are." He handed the paper back to her. "Yes, you'd be quite correct ending your journey here."

She thanked him nicely for the information. His words echoed in her mind as she helped the children gather their belongings. But their journey wasn't really ending. It was actually just beginning.

Twenty minutes later, Emma and the children stood alone on an empty platform. They'd watched as the other passengers were met and then as the station slowly emptied. She didn't see a sign of Andrej amongst the departing passengers, but he could easily have disembarked at an earlier station.

Lily and Peter's anxious glances her way didn't go unnoticed. She smiled at them reassuringly, although she didn't feel altogether confident herself. What on earth was she to do if no one came to collect them?

Fortunately, she didn't have to cross that bridge. Not five minutes later, a portly gentleman wrapped in an overcoat with no hat covering his gray hair hustled toward them. He smiled a cheerful smile and Emma felt instantly reassured as he stopped in front of them.

"Well, it looks as if you're all waiting here for me." He offered a handshake first to Lily, then Peter, and finally Emma. "I apologize for not meeting your train on time. I had to scare up some petrol." He looked at the children with a serious expression. "Tell me, am I forgiven?"

"It's not a problem, Sir," Lily assured him.

"Sir? Is there a sir around here?" The man spun in a small circle as if he were looking for someone else. The children giggled, and Emma couldn't help but smile at his good-natured antics. "The name's William Metcalf. It would please me greatly if you'd call me Uncle Will though. Does that sound agreeable to you two youngsters?"

The children nodded.

"This is Emma Bradley," Lily solemnly introduced her. Will and Emma shared an amused smile at Lily's formal demeanor. "Mummy said we're to mind Aunt Emma and the other adults we will be living with."

"And we're not to be any trouble," Peter added. "We promised Mum."

Emma and Will's eyes met. Unspoken sympathy for the children passed between them.

"I've no doubt that you'll be perfectly pleasant to have around," Will said. "My misses is anxious to meet you. Shall we head home?"

Home. The word sounded with angel's trumpets in Emma's mind. Home, even if it was someone else's home, sounded like a heavenly refuge. From the moment Patricia had been killed, and Emma had taken Patrick, she'd lived with a twisted, gnawing fear that she'd never be able to breathe easily again. She wasn't out of danger yet, she may never be again, but at least she might be able to catch her breath here.

They followed Will out of the station, through the car park, and toward his waiting Vauxhall. After he stowed their luggage, the children climbed into the back and Emma sank into the front seat with a sigh.

"Tired?" Will asked after they were underway.

"Anxious, actually," Emma replied. She looked over her shoulder, relieved to see the children were happily chattering away. "Although your warm welcome certainly has helped ease my mind."

"What about this little one?" Will nodded his head in the baby's direction. "Who is wrapped in the green blanket, is that your son or daughter there?"

Emma's stomach lurched. She knew the question was eventually going to be asked of her. The thought of lying made her ill but it had to be done. "This is Patrick."

"Shame that your husband had to miss the little one coming into the world," Will said. He glanced over at Emma. "I assume he's abroad? Let me guess, a naval man?"

Emma remained silent rather than offer forth one more lie. Practicing deception was more uncomfortable than she'd imagined it would be.

"I know it's difficult for you ladies with your young men gone," Will said. "It was the same during the last war." His gaze drifted to the rear view mirror. "Poor little ducks, it's horrible they've had to leave their mum, although they're probably safer here. They seem to be holding up well."

"They seem to be." Emma hoped she'd soon be able to say the same about herself. Getting out of London was all she had focused on for weeks, most of that time spent waiting with bated breath. Waiting for Malcolm to ring and taunt her that her time was up. Waiting for a knock on the door, wondering if the police had finally come round to take Patrick away.

"I smell the sea," Peter called out with delight.

"I can see the water now." Lily sounded equally thrilled.

Emma inhaled deeply and turned to smile at them. "Lovely, isn't it? Have you been to the seaside before?"

"No," Lily said. "May we swim today?"

"It's a bit cold for that." Will laughed, seemingly delighted by their enthusiasm. "Perhaps we have time for a quick look though." He pulled the car to a stop on the side of the road.

The children scrambled down the embankment and ran towards the water, waving back to Emma to acknowledge her words of caution. She leaned against the car and drew the edges of the baby's blanket to better cover a still sleeping Patrick.

"Thank you for stopping." She smiled her gratitude at Will, who stood a few feet away watching the children. "Lily and Peter looked so miserable this morning. It's wonderful to see them so happy."

Will shook his head ruefully. "My misses is looking forward to having little ones around. We'll do our best to see they are busy and comfortable until it's time for them to go home."

"I know their mother would be desperately grateful to hear you say so." Emma waved to a beaming Lily who was shrieking with delight as the waves rolled in, narrowly missing her shoes as she jumped back with each new wave. Peter was busy pitching stones into the water.

"Do you and Mrs. Metcalf have family in the area?" she asked. Her innate curiosity, her mother had often told Emma, was both her best and worst quality. Still, she was soon to be living amongst strangers and, with all the uncertainties in her life, the more she knew, the better she felt.

Will stood with his hands in his overcoat pockets, looking out at the sea without speaking.

"Forgive me for asking," Emma quickly said. Why must she constantly be asking so many questions? Her mind flashed back to the night before when she was walking with Andrej to Paddington Station. He'd not answered any of her questions.

"No need for apologies, Emma." Will turned to her, his countenance far more somber than it had been earlier. "Our only child was killed in the last war."

"I'm sorry." Emma snuggled Patrick even closer to her chest. "That must be an unimaginable sadness to bear."

"Yes, it is. I'm afraid my misses hasn't ever been quite the same," Will said. "It's been hard on both of us to watch the next generation of young lads go off to fight, knowing they won't all be coming home." They stood in somber silence for several moments. "Seeing as we'll never be grandparents, Joanna will be happy enough when she sees these three little ones."

"Having us won't be too painful for her?"

Will shook his head. "Just the opposite. We'll enjoy a house full of children."

Peter and Lily ran toward them, delighted smiles stretching across their rosy cheeks.

"The sea is brilliant, Aunt Emma." Peter's smile stretched across his face. "Will we be living close by?"

"We're not to far from home, my boy. Into the car you go, and I'll answer your questions as we drive." Will held open the door for Emma, and the children piled into the backseat. He put the Vauxhall into gear and pulled back onto the road. "You'll be living with me and the misses at Laurel Cottage, which is on the grounds of an estate called Laurel Manor."

"Who lives in the manor house, Sir?" Lily asked.

"You're supposed to call him Uncle William," Peter reminded her.

Emma turned round just in time to see Peter pull one of his sister's braids. She raised an eyebrow at him and he muttered a quiet apology to his sister.

"The RAF has requisitioned the Manor, Lily. The family who lived there has gone up to Scotland for the duration." Will slowed the car as they drove through what Emma assumed to be the Palace Pier area. The children joined her in staring out the windows as they made their way through Brighton.

"Are the planes close by, Uncle William?" Peter asked.

"Most are kept at the local RAF field. Only a few are on the Manor grounds. Don't worry, my boy, you'll see aircraft aplenty overhead."

"I want to see a dogfight with the Luftwaffe."

The excitement in her brother's voice was apparently more than Lily could take. She groaned loudly and flopped back against the seat, her arm flung over her eyes.

"Peter, you are the only one who wants to see that kind of action this close to England," Emma scolded him. "The rest of us prefer quiet skies. So let's have enough of that talk for now." She turned to Will, determined to change the subject. "What else can you tell us about Laurel Cottage?"

"Joanna will give you a proper look round when we get there, of course. You and the children have rooms up on the first floor. Our room is on the ground floor. As well, your immediate supervisor will be living with us." He glanced over at her. "Do you know him well?"

Emma shook her head. "No, not at all actually. I certainly had no idea we'd be living in the same house."

"Not to worry, my dear," Will reassured her. "We've plenty of room and the billeting officer thought it made proper sense for you both to be close to the Manor. That is where his offices will be."

"Have you met him?"

"Not yet. He was due in on the same train you lot were but he sent word that he'd be making a few stops in town to check on books and supplies he'd ordered."

"Do you know his name?" Emma asked. Forewarned was forearmed, as her father used to be fond of saying.

"Let's see now if I can remember how to pronounce it." Will thought for a moment. "It's a Dutch name, I remember that much."

Emma's eyes widened. Surely not.

"I say, that's a coincidence," Peter leaned forward from the back seat. "We met a Dutch man on the train."

"Yes, and Peter came up with a theory about him." Lily grinned at her brother. "What did you think he was, Peter?"

"I know what I think you are, Lily," he muttered in a low voice before turning back to the adults. "Our chap was named Mr. Van der Hoosen."

Will grinned. "One and the same I'd say. I'm glad you've had a chance to get acquainted. What a great bit of luck."

Luck? Emma fervently hoped that truly it was coincidence. Otherwise, it might mean that Andrej's presence had something to do with Malcolm.

She focused on the passing landscape and listened half-heartedly as Will and the children chatted. She concentrated on breathing evenly and keeping her galloping heartbeat under control. All along she'd known that one uphill battle after another awaited her as she fought to keep Malcolm away from Patrick. If Andrej was associated in any way with Malcolm, she'd have to find out straight away and then turn the situation to her advantage. She continued gazing out the window as they drove, trying to ignore the fact that the sky overhead was the exact color of a certain Dutchman's eyes.

ANDREJ WASN'T A DRINKING MAN. AFTER THE DAY HE'D HAD, HOWEVER, he could well stand a pint. When he spotted the Green Dog Pub, he made straight for it and requested a Guinness.

The young woman behind the bar made a face. "We're not serving anything Irish, and quite rightly so. If the Irish want to stay neutral then they can keep their lager to themselves." She pulled a draft of a lighter ale and set the mug before Andrej. "If Eamon de Valera drinks himself to death while we're fighting the Nazis, it's no more than he deserves."

Rather than speak, Andrej simply nodded. If she wanted to take that as his tacit approval of her political views as well, she could. The Green Dog was nearly empty; a handful of old men in the midst of a chess game by the window were the only other occupants. The barmaid watched him from the corner of her eye, but Andrej avoided her gaze. Conversation with a woman was the last thing he wanted.

Meeting Emma again on the train had unnerved him. Seeing her had also intrigued him, more than he cared to admit. She appeared to be every bit as smart and capable as she was beautiful. Her manner with Peter and Lily had been so natural that it was hard to believe she wasn't their mother. Certainly, there was no mistaking how deeply devoted to her son she was. The way she cradled him against her, it was as if she was holding on to him for dear life. Andrej drained the last of his lager.

"Shall I draw you another?" the barmaid asked.

"No, thank you." Andrej shook his head and placed a few coins on the counter. "Could you direct me to the nearest taxi queue?"

"Old Mr. McAffie will take anyone anywhere for a few shillings. You'll find him down at the end of the street beside the newsstand. If he's not there just wait, he'll be back shortly." She pocketed the money. "Will you be staying in Brighton long?"

Andrej shrugged. He didn't do well when strangers questioned him. He thought of Peter and smiled ruefully. "I'm not certain." He turned to leave but then curiosity got the better of him. He turned back. "Have you heard of a place called Laurel Cottage?"

"Aye, it is a little cottage on the edge of the Laurel Manor estate." She moved off to tend to a new arrival but called over her shoulder, "It should suit you well enough if you don't mind the quiet."

Quiet was just what he wanted. Andrej thanked her and headed in search of the newsstand. Laurel Cottage sounded like the ideal place to put Emma out of his mind.

CHAPTER 4

*A*s the taxi drove past Laurel Manor and wound its way through the grounds towards the cottage, Andrej's spirits lightened. All distractions aside, notably his thoughts of Emma, he looked forward to learning more about the work awaiting him. He knew precious little about the details. All that mattered to him was that he was not going to be 'Andrej, the world renowned concert pianist' but instead a regular man with a job that supported the war effort. A rare smile crossed his face as he handed Mr. McAffie the fare.

After the taxi pulled away, Andrej stood and looked up at the place he now would call home. Laurel Cottage was built of granite which sparkled in the mid-day sun. The lattice windows were framed by late summer rambling roses threaded through trellises on either side. The window boxes were painted the same forest green color as the front door before him.

He'd never imagined having a home of his own, seeing no point in dwelling on what wasn't meant to be. If he had, though, this would have been exactly the type of home he'd have wished for.

He rapped the brass door knocker with a deep sense of content-ment. At last, a peaceful place to live was before him. A job that mattered awaited him. He only needed someone to answer his knock and his new life would begin.

He glanced down at the threshold just as the door opened. He found himself looking at the most enchanting pair of ankles he'd ever seen.

"Hello."

He sucked in a sharp breath as the familiar voice greeted him. But it couldn't be Emma. What would she be doing here? Surely this was a trick, his subconscious mind's revenge for his earlier preoccupation with thoughts of her.

"Welcome to Laurel Cottage, Andrej," she said. "We've been expecting you."

Andrej raised his eyes. Emma. Framed in the doorway, she was no less lovely than he remembered. Something was different about her though. Her eyes. Yes, that was it. In spite of her pleasant tone, there was a challenge, a question, in them that he hadn't seen before.

"Emma," he held her gaze without looking away. "What are you doing here?"

"The children and I will be living here with you." She smiled and leaned against the door frame. "Apparently, I'm to be your new secretary."

"Hello, Mr. Van der Hoosen," a voice called from above Andrej's head. He took a step back to get a better look. Peter and Lily leaned out an upstairs window, frantically waving a cheerful greeting. Good God. The cottage was shrinking before his eyes.

"Isn't this a fantastic piece of luck, Sir?" Peter called down.

"Unbelievable, Peter," Andrej managed to choke out. "Truly unbelievable."

"You'd best come in." Emma stood back and held the door open. "I'll introduce you to our host and hostess, a Mr. and Mrs. Metcalf."

Andrej looked down at the threshold and willed his feet to move. Stepping into the cottage was to enter a new world, and not the quiet secluded one that he had been envisioning. Entering the cottage meant constantly having children around, it doubtless meant meals taken together, complete with conversations about how everyone's day had been. It meant living like they were a family. His insides tightened.

He couldn't continue to stand there staring at the threshold as if it were a ring of fire lest Emma think he was completely daft. Andrej took a deep breath and picked up his suitcases. Although he'd never lived in such close proximity to others before, he'd have to find a way to survive the experience. Heaven help him.

Twenty minutes later, Andrej closed the door to what was to be his new room and heaved a sigh of relief. His meeting with the Metcalfs had been pleasant enough. Both Will and Joanna had greeted him warmly and not asked any personal questions, which he'd taken as a hopeful sign.

He sank down on the small single width bed, ignoring its groan as it registered his large frame. Laurel Cottage, while solidly built and impeccably maintained, was like most other English cottages built in the same era, with low ceilings, narrow hallways, and tiny rooms. His room was on the ground floor near the front of the house, while Emma and the children would be up on the first floor. Perhaps that degree of separation would go a long way to providing him the privacy he wished for.

A knock at his door disproved the theory. Andrej opened the door, mindful not to hit his head on the low beams.

"Hello, Sir." It was Peter, with Lily beside him.

Andrej nodded a greeting. The expectant looks on the children's faces warned him that a nod wasn't enough, he'd need to use words. He took a deep, calming breath.

"Peter, Lily," he tried again, and was rewarded with two smiles.

"Aunt Emma asked us to fetch you for tea," Lily said.

"Please thank her for me. However, I will not be joining you." He started to close the door but stopped. Neither child had moved. "Is there something else you wish of me?"

Peter nodded.

Andrej waited.

"It's like this, Sir," Peter finally said. "Our mum told us to mind the adults, especially when we are asked to help."

"Admirable."

"So that means you'll just have to come with us," Lily said. "The longer we wait for you the colder the tea will become."

Andrej closed his eyes for just a moment and opened them again. No. The walls weren't actually closing in on him. He looked from Peter's intent gaze to Lily's hopeful expression and sighed. Refusing such eager little faces was so much easier in theory than practice.

"Lead the way," he heard himself say. Tomorrow would be soon enough to start avoiding Emma and the children.

Joanna and Emma, with Patrick snuggled in her arms, were already seated at the round farmhouse table when Andrej and the children entered the kitchen. He returned their greetings as he settled into the chair furthest from Emma.

Moments later, as he sipped his tea and tasted a fish paste sandwich that Lily proudly told him she'd made herself, Andrej realized that there were blessings to be found at Laurel Cottage. Greatest among these was the fact that Joanna Metcalf could not only keep up with Peter's chatter, but he'd wager the older woman could actually out talk him. Which meant that he would be free to sit in the relative safety of silence.

"Forgive us, Mr. Van der Hoosen," Joanna said, barely a moment later. "I didn't mean to exclude you from our conversation."

"No offense taken, be assured," Andrej said. "Please continue."

Joanna passed the plate of sandwiches to a grateful looking Peter, who had been sitting quietly and staring at his empty plate. "No, my goodness, I've been rude enough. Please tell us about yourself."

"I'd much prefer you continue with your conversation," Andrej hedged. He glanced at Peter. This would be the ideal time for one of Peter's interruptions, but the boy was busy polishing off one sandwich after another.

"Does your family live in England or are they still in Holland?" Joanna asked. "Peter told us that you were Dutch."

As many times as he had been asked this in the past, Andrej was always unprepared for the way his words caught in his throat when he tried to speak of the family he'd never known. Hitler's invasion of

Holland in May had people all the more concerned about his family's welfare, but answering the questions didn't become easier with practice.

"Communication between England and the Continent being what it is, I have no idea how things are in Holland." Andrej felt the eyes of both women upon him but neither spoke. He shrugged. "I have no family in England."

"No wife or children, Sir?" Lily asked.

Andrej looked down into her sympathetic little brown eyes. He shook his head wordlessly, hopeful that this would signal his desire for a change of subject.

Joanna sat quietly staring at him for a moment. Doubtless, she too felt sorry for him. It was a common enough reaction among women, which was exactly the reason he detested this line of questioning.

"Surely you must still have relations of some sort in The Netherlands?" Emma asked.

Andrej stiffened at the slight challenge in her voice. "Not anyone that I know of, Emma."

"Where do your parents live now if not in England or Holland?" she persisted.

"I can well ask you the same." He looked her straight in the eye, hoping to match the challenge in her voice.

"Canada. They emigrated three years ago to Ontario. I chose to stay in England."

Andrej frowned. Why on earth had Emma asked him to take her baby to an orphanage if she'd been killed in the bombing if she had a family? Hadn't she said she was alone in the world? Perhaps she wasn't in contact with her parents. He, of all people, should understand that having blood relatives wasn't the same as having a family.

"Your husband didn't want to emigrate as well?" Joanna asked.

Peter's head snapped up in surprise. "Aunt Emma isn't married."

All eyes turned to him. Lily's expression mirrored the surprise on Joanna's face.

Joanna fixed a stern expression on him. "Now, young man, what makes you say a crazy thing like that?"

"She doesn't wear a wedding ring." Peter pointed to Emma's left hand.

Joanna waved a hand dismissively. "That hardly means anything, Peter. Not all women fancy wearing jewelry."

"Peter's correct." Emma looked around the table, head held high with no trace of apology in her voice. "I've never been married."

Andrej set his tea cup down in the saucer with a decided clink. He avoided looking at Emma, although he was certain his surprise was evident. She was unmarried but that didn't mean she was unattached. Not with a baby as young as Patrick.

"Does our mum know?" Lily asked.

Emma nodded. "Yes, she does, Lily."

"That's all right then," Peter chimed in. He pushed back his plate and stretched his arms wide. "I thought perhaps I'd take a nap now."

"I thought perhaps we'd go in to Brighton and register you two for school so you may start straight away." Emma smiled at him. "I like my idea better."

"School?" Peter flopped back in his chair, an incredulous expression on his face.

"Term has just started, Peter," Emma reminded him. She took an empty bottle from Patrick's mouth and shifted him to her shoulder. She gently patted his back. "Your mum must have told you that you'd both be attending school while you were here."

"Perhaps she did mention it," Peter conceded.

"Don't be daft, Peter," Lily scolded him. "You know full well Mum and Granny told us that we would go to school here."

Andrej watched Lily frown at her brother. Peter shrugged the disapproval off as if it were commonplace. The exchanges between the two intrigued Andrej. Despite the occasional recriminations, their fondness for each other was evident.

He sat back in his chair and let his gaze settle on the bird sitting on the windowsill. Did he have brothers or sisters? Shadowy images of three children flitted across his mind's eye. Was he one of the children? Were the other two his siblings? The memory was disquieting, as always, and he pushed it away. The past held nothing for him.

A knock at the cottage door interrupted the conversation and brought Andrej back from his thoughts of the past. Joanna excused herself and returned just moments later.

"Emma, Doctor Graves has dropped by to take a look at Patrick." Joanna raised an eyebrow. "He says you phoned his surgery?" She let the question hang in the air.

Emma stood and pushed back her chair. Patrick let out a wail, not pleased at being disturbed. "Ssshh," Emma soothed him. "Thank you, Joanna. I'll come straight through."

"Is the baby ill?" Joanna persisted.

"No, he's fine. I just wanted to consult with the doctor about something." Emma turned her attention to the children, speaking in a quiet, rational manner despite Patrick's increasingly loud cries. Andrej marveled at her patience. "Lily and Peter, please go wash up before we leave for town."

When Emma left the room, he followed behind, intent upon returning to his room. A few steps behind them, Peter and Lily raced out of the kitchen, down the hallway, practically flying around the corner and up the stairs. Worried they would knock into Emma, Andrej reached out and steadied her as they passed.

He released his hold quickly as the children dashed up the stairs, each trying to reach the landing first.

"Forgive me, Emma," he apologized.

She turned to look up at him. "Please don't apologize, Andrej. You've been so kind from the moment you first found me in London. I daresay I could get quite spoiled having you always ready to keep me from harm." She smiled at him, a smile that sent a rush of warmth around his heart. "For the moment though, I need to remind them that running in the house is not acceptable."

She started toward the stairs but Joanna came out of the kitchen, wiping her hands on a dish towel. "You'd best go through to the sitting room and speak with Doctor Graves. I'll set the little ones straight."

Joanna took several steps up the staircase but then stopped to lean over the railing. "I'll try to sound stern but it's not easy. It's so lovely to have children in the house." With a warm smile, she continued her climb.

"Please do be firm, Joanna," Emma called after her. "I enjoy quiet afternoons like this and don't want those two getting ideas that we'll tolerate racing indoors."

Quiet afternoons like this? There hadn't been a quiet moment the entire meal. Yet, Andrej had to admit, the afternoon hadn't been altogether unpleasant, despite his expectations to the contrary.

EMMA SAT AND WATCHED DR. GRAVES AS HE EXAMINED THE BABY. Under other circumstances, she would be impressed with the doctor. His manner was professional yet kind, he listened attentively, and his touch with the baby was gentle. His eyes were too shrewd for Emma's comfort though. She stood, crossed her arms and chewed pensively on her lip. How long was this going to take?

"I'm pleased to say this little gentleman appears to be in wonderful health," the doctor said as he folded the edges of the blanket until Patrick was tightly swaddled. He cradled the baby in the crook of his arm instead of handing him back to Emma. Instead, he motioned for her to sit on the loveseat.

Emma sat back down, struggling to keep her impatience and worry hidden. She took a deep, steadying breath.

"My secretary told me that you're looking for a wet nurse."

Emma nodded but said nothing. Perhaps if she tried to look embarrassed the doctor would take pity on her and hurry this interview along.

He didn't. Emma answered his questions as best she was able, which was no easy task considering she knew nothing about breastfeeding. She tried to artfully dodge his questions about the baby's delivery. To her ears, she sounded half-witted but certainly that was better than sounding guilty.

"I'd like to prescribe something that will increase your milk flow."

Emma's eyes widened. She hadn't anticipated this.

Dr. Graves misunderstood her reaction. "I assure you, Mrs. Bradley, that you needn't be embarrassed about this. You would be surprised how many women need a little assistance with nursing. This herbal remedy usually does wonders within a few weeks."

"Yes, of course, fine then." Emma said, seeing her agreement as a way to shorten the interview. She had no intention of taking any herbal remedies. "In the meantime, though, Dr. Graves, what am I meant to do for Patrick?"

He gently handed the baby back to Emma. "There is a young woman who lives not far from here who is willing to act as a wet nurse. She's nursing her fifth child now. Iris Morrison is her name. Joanna knows her well enough to introduce you to her." He took a pad from his satchel, quickly scribbled out a script, and handed it to her. "The chemist should have this in his shop and can answer any questions you might think of. Don't hesitate to ring my surgery if you have questions, my dear."

Emma accepted the offered script and slipped it into her pocket as she thanked the doctor and saw him out of the cottage. She'd visit the chemist, pay for the herbs, and dispose of them just as quickly. She closed the front door and leaned against it, limp with relief.

Everything would be fine. The baby was safely in her arms, she'd found a wet nurse, and Patrick would have the nutrition he needed. She'd dodged yet another bullet today, which was what she'd have to do, one after the other, as she continued her charade.

Joanna waved from the cottage's front door to a departing Peter and Lily as they followed Emma around the bend of the drive on their way to the bus stop. She smiled as she heard the back door leading to the kitchen slam shut.

"Where are Emma and the little ones headed?" Will asked as he leaned against the wall and pulled off his boots.

"Into town to register Peter and Lily for school." Purely by habit, Joanna scooped up her husband's boots and tossed them into the mud room as Will washed his hands at the sink. She gestured to the table where Will's tea was laid out for him. "The children are lovely."

Will returned his wife's smile as he filled his cup. "I tell you what's lovely, that smile on your face." He took a long sip of tea. "You didn't want to keep the baby here with you?"

"Of course, I wanted to. I offered but Emma adamantly refused."

Will shrugged. "Natural enough for a new mother to not want her babe out of sight, I suppose."

Joanna hesitated, just a moment too long to escape her husband's notice.

"Out with it, Jo." He settled back into his chair and crossed his arms, an expectant look on his face. "Is it Emma or Andrej that's put that worried look in your eyes?"

She pulled out a chair and sat down opposite her husband. She sighed deeply. "You know me so well."

"I should hope so after all these years." He winked at her playfully and then reached across the table to squeeze her hand. "What's wrong?"

"Nothing is wrong exactly. I think Mr. Van der Hoosen seems—"

Will held up his hand. "Wait, why do you call him by his surname? He specifically asked us to call him Andrej."

"I know but there's something about him that makes that not seem proper somehow. It's hard to explain. It's almost as if he belongs on a stage. Not like an actor or anything dodgy. But when he walks in a room, it's as if a performance is about to begin. He has that air about him. Silly, isn't it?"

Will shook his head. "No, not silly at all. Perhaps he's a professor." He shrugged. "Are you uncomfortable with him living here?"

Joanna smiled at the tender expression in her husband's eye. "No, not at all. He appears to be very courteous and respectful, quiet too. No, it's not him. It's Emma."

Will's eyebrows shot up. "Did you two have words?"

"No, don't be daft. Nothing like that."

Will waited for her to continue.

Joanna was reluctant to confess to her husband that she'd looked

41

at Emma's ration book when Emma had run back upstairs to fetch her hat. The ration book had been right there, on the table under a pair of gloves. It caught Joanna's eye only because it was the wrong color. Pregnant women and nursing mothers were issued green books, but Emma's was decidedly a buff color. She'd taken a quick peek inside and, turning it cover to cover, saw no mention of Patrick. He should have been registered in Emma's book. This wasn't the ration book of a woman who had given birth recently, or one who had an infant. It made no sense.

She met her husband's expectant gaze. No, she wouldn't tell him. He'd consider her curiosity to be snooping. "Emma isn't married."

"Fancy that."

"You're not shocked?"

Will shrugged. "It's unfortunate, certainly. But plenty of young girls got themselves in the same trouble during the last war. Why should this war be any different?" Will refilled his tea cup, sat back in his chair, and studied her. "I can't see how it's any of our business when it comes right down to it."

Joanna decided the conversation was taking a turn she wasn't comfortable with. Despite what her husband seemed to be implying, she wasn't being judgmental. She liked Emma.

As the conversation shifted toward Will's morning work at the Manor, questions continued to tumble round her mind. Why wasn't Emma nursing her baby? Surely the scarcity of powdered formula, not to mention the expense, would be a burden? Why wasn't Patrick registered in his mother's ration book? And the biggest question of all, if Emma wasn't married, who was Patrick's father?

CHAPTER 5

a piercing wail broke through Andrej's sleep. Dazed, he sat up, listening to the shrill cries of the air raid siren. He rubbed his hands over his face, willing his mind to understand why the siren sounded different. As his eyes adjusted to the moonlit room, he remembered where he was. What he was hearing wasn't a siren at all, someone was crying. Screaming.

He hesitated only a moment before he grabbed his dressing gown. He shrugged into it as he left his room. But halfway up the stairs, he paused in the shadows. What was he doing getting involved? The cries weren't those of a baby, they sounded like a child's cry. What comfort could he bring to a child? His mind willed him to go back to his room but the cries he heard triggered memories that anchored him to the stairs.

Andrej looked up as Emma flung open her door. He watched as she paused in the hallway only long enough to identify where the cries were coming from. She rushed toward Lily and Peter's door, eased it open, and disappeared into their room without hesitating. The immediacy of her actions propelled him forward. The second to the last step groaned under his weight as he reached the landing. After a brief hesitation, he stood just outside the children's door. Close enough to see and hear, he stayed where he could safely observe without being seen.

∾

BRIGHT MOONLIGHT FILLED THE ROOM. PETER SAT UP IN BED, RUBBING his eyes. Emma hurried to Lily's bedside and bent over the sobbing child. Lily whimpered as she flailed from side to side, fighting to free herself from the tangle of blankets.

"Lily, everything's all right," Emma called softly as she gently shook the little girl's shoulder. "Wake up, love."

"Aunt Emma?" Peter called out from his bed on the other side of the room. "What's happening?" He sounded wide awake. "What's the matter with my sister?"

Emma placed a hand on Lily's forehead. She was relieved that the girl didn't feel feverish. "She's fine, Peter. Lay back down. It's only a bad dream."

Emma sat on the edge of the bed and tried to rouse Lily. Lily's cries quieted to whimpers and, after a few moments, she opened her eyes. She looked wildly about the room before her eyes settled on Emma. "I want Mummy," Lily sobbed.

Emma held out her arms and gently drew the little girl closer. Her heart heavy with sadness, she cradled Lily, all the while making soothing sounds.

"You'd best stop your fussing, Lily. You can't have Mummy," Peter said matter-of-factly from across the room. "And you can't have Daddy either. Or Granny."

"Hush now, Peter," Emma scolded him. "Of course she can. Just not tonight, that's all."

"Are you certain about that, Aunt Emma?" Lily straightened and looked up at Emma with wide eyes. "Absolutely certain we can go home?"

"I'm absolutely, positively certain." Emma smiled reassuringly as she reached out to dry Lily's tears. "When the war is over, and life goes back to normal, you and Peter will be at home with your parents and your granny."

As soon as the words were out of her mouth, it occurred to Emma that the war *was* normal to the children. They were hardly old enough to remember what it had been like before air raids, bombing, and food shortages reached Britain.

"I miss Mummy so much." Lily rubbed her eyes sleepily. "In my dream I was trying to get to her, but I couldn't find my way. It was foggy and I got lost." Her lower lip started to tremble.

"Your mum misses you just as much. In fact, I'm willing to bet that she's laying awake in her bed at home right this very moment thinking of you both."

"She's not," Peter piped up from the other side of the room. "Mummy works nights at the hospital and sleeps during the day. Unless there are day time raids, then she doesn't sleep at all. Usually we stay with Granny during the day."

Emma looked over to where Peter lay in bed. He had his arms folded behind his head, looking perfectly wide awake. Could children be nocturnal? She hoped not.

She turned back to Lily, who appeared calmer than she had moments ago.

"Let's think about this then. If your mum is awake at night, she'll be missing you then. And your Granny will be missing you during the day when she's awake. So, no matter what time it is, day or night, someone will be thinking of you every moment. Does that sound about right?"

"It sounds lovely," Lily said. She lay back down and snuggled into her pillow, her smile a valiant effort to appear brave.

Emma stood and straightened her blankets. "Snug enough?"

"Snug enough," Lily concurred. She covered her mouth as she yawned.

"What about Daddy?" Peter asked.

Emma sighed. Children, she was rapidly learning, could ask very complicated questions. "What about him, Peter?"

"When will he be missing us?"

Emma hesitated. She knew nothing about the children's father, and she was afraid to say the wrong thing. Still, she knew she needed to say something to reassure him. "I'm very sure that he is thinking of you all, Peter, wherever he is, whatever time it is."

Peter looked at Emma intently. "How can you know that, Aunt Emma? Really know that, I mean?"

Emma crossed over to the bed. She pulled the blankets up to his chin and tucked them around him securely before looking down at his serious little face. "I can tell you this, Peter, a mother is always thinking of her child, always loving them, wherever they are. Always, always, always."

Emma sat down on the edge of Peter's bed. Both children seemed to be waiting for her to continue. She had no idea what to say next. In truth, there were no words to ease their worries completely. They had more questions than she had answers.

"What about a father?" Peter asked. "Does a father always love his son?"

Emma's stomach clenched as Malcolm's face appeared before her eyes. She shut them against the image. Nothing she could do, however, could erase the memory of his words when he'd first seen Patrick. "That bloody bastard is of no more consequence to me than his gutter whore of a mother". Malcolm wasn't a father. He was a curse. But that wasn't what the children were asking about. "Yes, of course, your father loves you and is thinking of you every moment, bar none. I'm beyond certain about that."

She decided it was time to change the subject. "Now, tell me what you think of Laurel Cottage."

The children exchanged telling glances.

"Of course, I know it isn't home." Emma clarified her question. "Will it do though while we wait to go back to London?"

"Oh, absolutely yes," Lily answered. "As long as we can go home again one day soon then we'll be fine here. Isn't that so, Peter?"

"Yes, Lily." Peter sounded curiously subdued, his agreement with his sister suspiciously swift.

"What is it, Peter?" Emma asked.

He was silent a moment. He looked searchingly at Emma before he spoke, his words thoughtful.

"You say we can eventually go home, Aunt Emma. And I believe Mum when she said she'd send for us when the bombing stops, but she doesn't really have any control over that, does she?" He sat up in bed and propped his pillow behind his back. "Daddy promised he would stay safe but now he's gone missing."

They sat in silence. Emma was unable to speak for the lump in her throat. Her first instinct was to throw out reassuring platitudes but she stopped herself. The children were smart enough to see through her empty promises, and heaven knew she had lied enough lately to last a lifetime. "Neither of your parents could guarantee the promise they made you, Peter. But they're telling you what they wish to be true. When I promise you can go home, I really mean I promise that I'll do everything in my power to make that happen. Does that make any sense?"

Peter nodded gravely and Lily followed his lead. Emma stood and crossed to the door. "Is there anything else you want to ask me before we all go back to sleep?"

"What's for breakfast?" Peter asked.

Lily giggled.

"Don't be cheeky, young man." Emma couldn't help but smile. "Goodnight, Peter. Goodnight, Lily. Sweet dreams."

Emma gingerly closed their door and then went back to her room. "Is all well?"

She let out a startled cry at the sound of Andrej's voice so near to her. She looked up at him, her eyes wide. They stood only a couple of feet apart.

"Forgive me, Emma. I didn't meant to startle you."

She drew the lapels of her dressing gown closed. "I didn't see you there." She waited for him to come forward but he remained where he was.

"I heard one of the children crying, yes?"

She nodded.

"They are fine now?" he asked.

"Yes, I daresay they're already drifting back to sleep. Lily had a nightmare. I'm sorry your sleep was disturbed."

"Not at all," he dismissed her concern. "The children have had a long, tiring day."

Emma found it difficult to tear her gaze away from his. Standing there in the semi-dark with Andrej didn't make her nervous, but it did leave her unnerved. A distinction that made little sense to her. "They have. We all have."

Andrej studied her as if he was truly seeing her for the first time. His expression was inscrutable. "Goodnight, Emma," he said, his voice deep and low. "Sleep well." Without waiting for a response, he turned and made his way down the stairs.

Emma watched him disappear. Only after she heard his bedroom door quietly close, did she enter her own room. She closed the door and leaned against it, willing her heart rate back to normal. After it slowed, she crossed over to the cot and straightened Patrick's blankets. Considering how loud Lily's cries had been, it was a miracle that the baby hadn't woken. She leaned in and brushed a soft kiss across his cheek before she climbed into bed.

But sleep eluded her as she lay staring up at the ceiling. If first impressions were anything to go by, Will and Joanna appeared to be good people. Laurel Cottage exceeded her expectations, and the luxury of a quiet night without hearing the air raid sirens wasn't one she took for granted.

Andrej's presence, however, was something she couldn't easily dismiss from her mind. He had saved her from the soldiers in the street, she owed him her gratitude for that. On the train, he'd saved her from spilling scalding hot water on herself and the baby, for which she was deeply appreciative. Even just now, when he'd come to see if Lily was alright, he'd been nothing but a gentleman.

But was it really a coincidence that they ended up working and living together? Malcolm couldn't possibly be behind Andrej's presence at Laurel Cottage, could he? As she drifted off into sleep, warmed by the down-feather-filled duvet atop her bed, and comforted knowing that Patrick was safely asleep only a few feet away, Emma fervently wished that fate alone, and not Malcolm's machinations, had brought Andrej to Laurel Cottage.

～

EMMA AWOKE FROM A SURPRISINGLY REFRESHING SLEEP NOT LONG AFTER the sun rose. She made every effort to be quiet as she bundled the baby and made her way down the stairs. Easing open the front door, she stopped to listen for signs that anyone else was up. Today she was due at Laurel Manor to report for work but first she needed to meet the woman Dr. Graves had recommended as a wet nurse. Concentrating on work was going to be impossible if she had to worry about Patrick being hungry.

The night before, when Emma had asked about Iris Morrison, Joanna had assured her that Iris was a lovely girl. How much of a girl she could be considered when she already had five children, Emma couldn't imagine. Will and Joanna had just laughed and shared a smile when Emma asked just that.

Mixed emotions tumbled round in both Emma's heart and head as she quickly made her way down the lane and past Laurel Manor to the Morrison's home. To her relief, it was close, and several quick trips a day back and forth would easily be feasible.

Will had told her to look for the house with a red gate and an ivy covered iron fence with at least one child dangling over it. Sure enough, the red gate materialized in front of her. Just as he'd said, a young girl was draped over the fence. Emma slowed to a stop. "Hello."

"Hello, Ma'am," the girl said. "Have you come to see my mum?"

"If your mum is Mrs. Morrison, then yes, I have." Emma eyed the child. Her guess was that the girl couldn't be more than five years old. Long blond hair, while clean, tumbled round her small face haphazardly. Curious blue eyes watched Emma in turn. "Will you please tell your mum that I would like to see her?"

"What is your name, Ma'am?" the girl asked.

"Miss Bradley."

The girl slipped down off the fence in a manner which told Emma that she'd done it many times before. Without a word, the girl raced back to the house, eased open the front door, and slipped in the house without a backward glance.

Emma looked over the cottage while she waited. The house appeared much as the girl had done, clean but untamed. The garden, however, was most definitely being tended to. A very good thing considering all the mouths Iris Morrison had to feed.

The front door opened and a different little girl, a slightly younger version of the first, waved for her to come in. She politely held the door open as Emma entered the cottage. "Mum is in the nursery with my baby brother but she'll be done shortly. Can you please wait in the front room?"

"I will, thank you." Emma followed the barefoot child through a doorway into a bright, cheerful, but overwhelmingly disorganized room. The morning sun shone through the windows, not a speck of dust to mar the brilliance of the light. Freshly cut roses in a porcelain pitcher rested on a low wooden table which showed nary a smudge of dirt. She smiled as the young girl cleared a stack of books and papers from a chair for her. Emma's curiosity was roused. What sort of woman lived in such chaotic cleanliness?

She barely had time to sit down and unwrap Patrick's blanket before she found out.

"Lovely to meet you, Miss Bradley. Lovely, just lovely," Iris said as she sailed in the room. Sailed was the proper word to describe her entrance too. Iris appeared to be just a bit older than Emma but twice, maybe three times as large, and as blond and fair as her daughters.

Iris bent over Patrick and caressed his tiny fist. Emma was relieved to see how gentle her touch was, that boded well for this working out. She was unprepared, though, for how quickly Iris scooped him up and out of Emma's arms before she could protest.

"There's a little love," Iris crooned as she settled onto the settee, only avoiding crushing a basket of paper dolls because one of her daughters snatched it out of the way in a practiced move and set it on top of a pile of wooden toys on the chair opposite her mother.

"So sorry to have kept you waiting, Miss Bradley. May I call you Emma? I just know we're to be fast friends and you're to call me Iris. We'll be seeing each other often enough trying to keep this little monster fed, won't we?"

"Please do call me Emma." She felt oddly comfortable with this whirlwind of a woman. "I appreciate you agreeing to meet me. I've been anxious to find a solution to my...dilemma."

Iris cradled the baby against her ample chest. "I've got enough milk coming in that I could be mistaken for a Jersey cow, but I've known other women who have had trouble. I'm happy to help out."

Iris' smile was so bright and her manner so genuine that Emma couldn't help but smile. Few women she'd ever met would refer to themselves as a cow, even in jest.

In less than an hour Emma was well versed on Iris Morrison's life. Despite the chaos, she could clearly feel the happiness in the household. Iris confessed to Emma that she'd set her sights on Robert Morrison, a much older widower with no children, when she'd been hired as his daily.

"I convinced him to give marriage another go. At first he wasn't all that keen but I'm a difficult woman to resist," Iris said with a wink. "Here we are seven years later with Roberta, Rachel, Rosemary, Roxanne, and finally our little Robert."

"Your husband is in the service?" Emma asked.

Iris laughed. "Goodness, no, he's too old. He's with the Civil Defense Fire Service in London. And here I thought one of the perks of being married to an older man was that he wouldn't have to go off to fight." She sighed. "Mind you, I was relieved he was only going to be in London and not some forsaken place like North Africa, but the wireless broadcasts from London have robbed me of that comfort. Is it really all that bad?"

Emma nodded. "Your husband's contribution is sorely needed."

The two women sat in silence for a long moment. Emma was glad

Iris didn't ask any additional questions. She didn't want to talk about bombs, fire, or the ensuing destruction right now.

Iris shifted Patrick to her other arm. "Now, tell about your young man."

Emma fidgeted in her chair. Confessing to being an unmarried mother had to get easier over time, didn't it? She'd be doing so for years to come so she'd best get used to it. "I'm not married."

"Yes, the 'Miss' in front of Bradley told me that, Emma." She nodded down at Patrick. "He didn't come through a fairy ring though, did he?" She met Emma's eyes. "But if you don't want to talk about it today, that's fine. There's always tomorrow."

For a moment, for ever so brief a second, Emma was tempted to confide in Iris. But a glance at Patrick strengthened her resolve to remain silent. Lies were the only way to keep them both safe.

That bullet dodged, the conversation turned to the reason she was there. They worked out a schedule whereby Emma would bring Patrick to Iris three times a day, morning, noon and night.

"I'll just stop round Laurel Cottage once a day for an extra feeding," Iris offered. "That way the children and I can get a nice walk in."

"I'll be working at the Manor during the day, and Patrick will be with me."

Iris waved her hand. "No matter, we can just as easily come there. Heaven knows there is room for my children to run wild while I'm feeding Patrick." She looked thoughtfully at Emma. "Does your supervisor know that you plan to have the baby with you while you work?"

"Not yet," she confessed. "That's my next hurdle."

Emma was relieved when Iris managed to get Patrick to nurse without too much trouble. The fear that he'd been too long on the bottle had niggled in the back of her mind. She gratefully accepted him back when Iris was done.

The baby lay snuggled against her chest as Emma waved goodbye to Iris and the children. She headed back to Laurel Cottage content in the knowledge that she had made a new friend in Iris. Emma considered herself a fairly good judge of character. Rarely did she question her instincts when she first met someone.

The thought of Malcolm flitted across her mind and she frowned. When she'd first met him, her stomach had curdled. He'd been far too cocky when he'd been introduced to the secretary pool, eyeing each woman in turn as if he was evaluating livestock. What he thought of as charm, she had found slick and unsettling. She only wished that her cousin, sweet trusting Patricia, had not been drawn in by him.

FROM THE LOWEST BRANCH OF THE TALLEST TREE IN THE YARD, PETER sat swinging his legs. He and Lily were meant to start school in a couple of hours. While he wasn't nervous exactly, neither was he as excited as his sister. He'd left her chattering away in the kitchen with Aunt Joanna and come in search of a quiet place.

He loved Lily, really he did, but every once in awhile he needed to get away from her. Besides, there were no trees this tall in London anywhere near their flat, and he'd always wanted to climb one.

Peter grew still when he heard the sound of crackling leaves below him. He leaned forward and peered down. Aunt Emma stood at the gate, gazing at the cottage as if she wasn't really seeing it. Adults could be so strange. He opened his mouth to call down to her but then decided against it. If Aunt Emma scolded him for being in the tree then perhaps he wouldn't be allowed to climb up it again. No, he'd best keep silent.

And then he heard Aunt Emma's voice. She was talking to Patrick, yet somehow the sound carried up to his ears. Not quite able to make out her words, Peter leaned forward and strained to hear.

A frown creased his forehead. Not Patrick's mother? Surely he hadn't heard that correctly. But no, Aunt Emma was telling the baby something about his mother. Peter leaned back and closed his eyes, wishing she would take Patrick inside the cottage. He felt like he'd been caught eavesdropping, but that wasn't right. He'd been here first. He opened his eyes again when he heard the door close. He counted to one hundred before he climbed down and walked slowly toward the cottage.

If Aunt Emma wasn't Patrick's mother, then who was? And why would she lie and say Patrick was her baby? That didn't make any sense, and Peter wanted to understand what he'd just heard. The only way to get a real answer was to ask an adult.

But which one?

CHAPTER 6

"*K*ill the bitch." Malcolm Shand-Collins held up a hand to forestall a protest from the private secretary who stood in front of his desk. He was out of patience and the morning was still young. It didn't bode well for the rest of the day going his way. "I don't want to be bothered with any of the details. Just get it done."

He turned his attention back to the paperwork on his desk and waited for the other man to leave the room.

"A bit drastic, wouldn't you say, Sir?" came a tentative protest that set Malcolm's teeth on edge. "Surely she doesn't have to die? There must be other options."

Why on earth was he constantly surrounded by people who were afraid of their own shadows? Mealy-mouthed, whimpering and weak. Lord, it felt like everyone around him was conspiring to destroy his last nerve.

"I don't want to hear one word about kindness, compassion, or other such rot." Malcolm threw down his pen and pushed his chair away from his desk. He crossed to the window and stared down into the garden of his country estate, an hour north of London. He should have stayed in the city, and he certainly should have known better than to try to work from home, surrounded as he was by idiots. His attention needed to be totally focused on his work. One slip could mean the noose.

And then there was the ever-pressing question about what to do about that bastard son of his. What was Emma's next move going to be? He frowned. He'd let her leave London with the baby without attempting to stop her because it suited his purposes to have the child out of sight.

He crossed to his desk and pulled open the bottom drawer. The revolver was cold to his touch but he welcomed the feel, the weight, the power of it. Reaching across the desk, he handed the weapon to his secretary.

"Take it," he snapped. "Get the job done."

"Did you want to say good-bye to her?"

Malcolm looked down at the Springer Spaniel standing quietly, tail wagging, her eyes intent upon him. Cursed nuisance. At least with her gone he'd not have to worry about tripping over her. She constantly followed him everywhere. He hated the feeling of being stalked.

"No." Malcolm waved the other man away. "Be done with it. We've got to see to all of this correspondence." He reached for the morning mail and slit open the first envelope.

Upon hearing the door close, he tossed the letter onto the desk, leaned back in his chair and closed his eyes. An image of Emma's face taunted him. The last time he'd seen her she had been full of threats. He had expected her anger. What he hadn't expected, however, was her defiance. Her eyes had held sparks of fire and she'd clutched the baby to her chest as if Malcolm were the devil himself. Her fury had been real, no question about that. But what of her threats? Did she have proof of his German associations or was she bluffing?

How had he been stupid enough to get trapped like this? No matter now, the trick was going to be getting through this without being caught. To his credit, he'd managed to eliminate Patricia and no one was the wiser. That meant he could do the same to Emma, but only with patience and planning. Perhaps, for now, it was wise to let her think she was free of him.

A shot rang out as Malcolm reached for the telephone. He didn't flinch as he asked to be connected to a number in Brighton.

~

EMMA KNOCKED ON THE DOOR TO HER NEW OFFICE AND PUSHED IT OPEN before anyone responded. She was late, not ideal on the first day, but she'd wanted to see Peter and Lily off to school herself.

"Good morning," she greeted the two men already in the room. "I apologize for being late." She smiled first at Andrej before she turned to the young airman standing opposite him. "I'm Emma Bradley."

"A pleasure to meet you, Mrs. Bradley." The young man smiled at her and shook her outstretched hand.

"It's Miss Bradley," Andrej corrected him before Emma had the chance to do so. "Emma, this is Flight Lieutenant Stuart Tollison. He's Wing Commander Blythe's assistant."

"I'm pleased to meet you, Lieutenant Tollison."

His smile was friendly. "Call me Stuart, please."

Andrej gave a pointed look at the clock. "You needn't worry you missed the Wing Commander, Emma. He's been called out to the air field."

"I wasn't worried at all," Emma answered with a smile. The day had started out far too nicely for her to grow cross with Andrej already. "I needed to see the children off to school." She turned her attention to the flight lieutenant, determined to change the subject. "Is this the room we'll be working in?"

The turn of topic was all that Stuart needed to launch into an account of their work space. Emma listened attentively as she followed him. He explained that the room that she and Andrej were to work in had previously been the conservatory. He stopped in front of a grand piano.

"We've cleared the room of the original owner's furniture but the piano itself was too large to remove." Stuart ran his fingers noisily over the keys. It didn't escape Emma's notice that Andrej cringed. "Of course, when W.C. Blythe learned Mr. Van der Hoosen would be working here the piano no longer seemed out of place."

Emma glanced at Andrej to see if he understood what Stuart meant but he didn't meet her eye. She turned back to Stuart. "Why do you say that?"

"It's nothing of significance," Andrej dismissed her question. "Lieutenant, I am most anxious to begin my first assignment. Do you have an idea when we can expect to meet with W.C. Blythe?"

"There's no telling, actually. His schedule is erratic on the quietest of days." He looked between them. "I can send word down to the cottage when he's on his way back if you'd prefer to wait there."

"No."

"No."

Both Emma and Andrej rejected the offer immediately, their refusals tripping over each other.

"I'm expecting someone to meet me here," Emma explained.

Stuart smiled broadly. "Right then. Let me just show you one more thing before I get back to work." He motioned to the broad expanse of glass windows that overlooked the Manor's south lawn. "This room isn't proofed for a black out. We'll be in tomorrow to install beaver board but the shape of the windows makes it impossible to achieve total darkness. Therefore, another room has been set aside for any work that you need to do after sundown. Let me show it to you."

Emma, with Andrej a step behind her, followed the young lieutenant to a set of carved oak doors off to the north side of the room. She stepped into a room as cozy as the conservatory was expansive, as comfortable a room as she could have wished for. It suited her needs perfectly.

There was only one small window, large enough to light the room but too narrow for anyone to fit through. She reached down to check the strength of the latch. Tight. Perfect. Silently she counted off a number of paces. Just right.

When she turned, she realized that Andrej was watching her. Fortunately, Stuart was still speaking so she went to his side. Her best guess was that Flight Lieutenant Tollison was around her age, perhaps a year or two older, but no more. However old he was, he seemed ages younger than Andrej. Between his cheerful demeanor, ready grin, and air of innocence, he had none of Andrej's watchful, weary manner.

"Is there anything else I can get for you before I leave?" Stuart asked.

"No, thank you, Lieutenant." Andrej walked towards the heavily carved wooden doors leading to the hallway and held one side open.

"Wait, Lieutenant Tollison--"

"Stuart, please."

Emma smiled warmly. "Yes, Stuart. I am expecting a delivery sometime today. Would it be possible for you to mention that to someone at the gate? I'm anxious not to miss it."

"Yes, of course, Miss Bradley--"

"Emma," she interrupted him. "It's only fair play."

Stuart nodded, looking pleased. "I'll send word down straight away, Emma." With another wide smile for her, and a brief nod to Andrej, he departed.

When the door shut behind him, Emma turned round to face Andrej. "Shall we begin?"

A raised eyebrow was his only answer. He studied her carefully, wordlessly, and Emma tried not to fidget under his scrutiny.

"Am I to know anything about this delivery of yours? Or the visitor you are expecting?"

His voice was low, controlled, and his accent eminently attractive, she decided. Yet the words he spoke were delivered in an even manner that didn't betray his thoughts. How did his voice sound when he was angry? Or happy? How did he sound first thing in the morning? She shook her head. That was a dangerous line of thought. He might well be attractive but that was all the more reason to keep her wits about her.

"Mr. McAffie's delivering a little something." She turned around and surveyed the room. Unlike the attached sitting room, the conservatory had been cleared of furniture and rugs and all that made the smaller room so welcoming. "I wonder why such a small room was built just off of this one?"

"I imagine it was intended to check proper acoustics. A room this size wouldn't give as true a sound as one like that."

Finally, Emma thought, here was a small piece of personal information about him. He knew something about music. She thought back to the reference Stuart had made earlier to Andrej and the piano. Of course, that was it. She grinned triumphantly. "You're a piano teacher, aren't you?"

His eyebrows rose. "What on earth are you talking about?"

"You haven't given me a single clue about what sort of work you did before the war." Emma was rather proud of herself for sorting it out. Judging by the look on Andrej's face, she'd hit close to the truth. Good.

"I'll admit I've been around a piano a time or two before," Andrej conceded. A wry smile tugged at the corners of his mouth. "Is there anything else you wish to know about me, Emma?"

Are you working for the man I hate? But, of course, she couldn't come right out and ask him. If Andrej was working for Malcolm, he'd lie about it. And if he, in fact, had no connection to Malcolm, her question would have given him information she didn't want him to have about her. "Not at the moment," she stepped around the truth. "Let's talk about the assignment at hand, shall we?"

A KNOCK ON THE GLASS DOORS BEHIND HIM STARTLED ANDREJ. HE turned from his makeshift desk and looked to see who wished to disturb him. His eyes widened at the sight of a large blond woman who frantically motioned for him to unlock the door. In one arm she cradled what looked to be a baby, and peeking out from behind her skirts were one, two, good heavens, was that a third child? A fourth, a slightly older girl, stood off to the side holding yet another baby.

Andrej sucked in a lungful of air. Surely this woman and her brood didn't plan on invading his office? He glanced over his shoulder but Emma still hadn't returned from her tour of the Manor. Young Lieutenant Tollison had stuck his head in the room more times that morning than Andrej could count. Each time he'd had a quick question to ask or a suggestion to make, his words directed at them both but his eyes had been for Emma only. Finally fed up with Tollison's blatant attempts to attract Emma's attention, Andrej had instructed her to join Stuart for a tour of the building, if for no other reason than to put the lad out of his misery.

Now Andjrej wished he hadn't been so impetuous. Emma would know how to handle this woman and her little entourage far better than he. He directed his attention back to the papers before him. Perhaps if he ignored the contingent they would just leave. After several long moments, he glanced back to see if they were still there. What he saw propelled him straight out of his chair. Four little curled fists were raised, ready to rap on the glass. He quickly crossed the room and pulled open the door.

"Took you long enough, my good man," the woman said as she pushed past him. The children followed quietly behind her, their curious eyes intent on his face. "We're here to see Miss Bradley."

Of course. This must be the visitor Emma said she was expecting. Why on earth had Emma not waited here for them? Oh, yes, he had sent her away.

"Miss Bradley is not here at the moment," Andrej said. "You are welcome to leave a note and I'll see she receives it."

"I am Iris Morrison." The woman waved her hand to indicate her little fair-haired charges. "These precious ones are my daughters." She leaned in towards Andrej and studied his face. "Ohhhh...you look familiar."

Andrej groaned inwardly. He had no idea who this woman was, but judging by the excitement dawning on her face, she recognized him.

"Andrej Van der Hoosen, the Andrej Van der Hoosen...as I live and breathe." She placed her free hand over her heart. "What a supreme treat this is to meet you." Her grin was wide. "My husband and I have gone to London to see you in concert, twice as it were. This simply is the most marvelous luck indeed to find you here."

"It's a pleasure to meet you, Madame." Andrej bowed slightly, eliciting giggles from the four little girls. Mercifully, the two babies weren't wailing. Andrej leaned in to take a closer look at the baby the oldest girl was holding. The blanket looked much like the one Emma kept Patrick wrapped in.

Was this woman to be Patrick's new nursemaid? Surely not, her hands were already more than full. Andrej realized that he hadn't thought to ask Emma what arrangements she'd made for her son while she worked.

"I've come to bring Patrick back to Emma," Iris answered his unspoken question.

"As I mentioned a moment ago, Miss Bradley isn't here just now." Andrej edged back towards the door and reached for the handle. "Shall I ask her to ring you when she's ready to fetch the child?"

Iris smiled broadly as she ignored the door he held open. Instead, she walked into the center of the cavernous room. "Won't you be kind enough to play just a bit for us, Mr. Van der Hoosen?" Iris stopped in front of the piano and lovingly ran her fingers over the top. "My particular favorite is Mozart's first sonata in C. Girls, gather around and listen."

"Unfortunately, I'm unable to accommodate you, Mrs. Morrison. I'm in the middle of an important project," Andrej lied.

"Nonsense."

"Pardon?" An inadequate response, but it was all he could manage through his surprise.

"Emma told me yesterday that this was to be your first day of work so I can't imagine what is so important already that you can't steal a few moments to gift us with your talent."

Andrej gave a discreet cough. "There is a war on, Mrs. Morrison." His response sounded more pompous than he meant it to, but, honestly, her presumption that she wasn't interrupting rankled.

"I'm fully aware there is a war on, Mr. Van der Hoosen. The meager rations I'm given to feed my children are a daily reminder." She lifted her chin and met his gaze straight on. "To my way of thinking, the circumstances in which we are forced to live is all the more reason to enjoy and appreciate beauty where we are able."

With that, Andrej couldn't argue. He glanced first at the piano, then at the door, and finally at the woman before him. He pulled out the bench and sat down in front of the keys. "Fair enough, Mrs. Morrison. The sonata you mentioned happens to be one of my favorites as well." He stretched his fingers and then flexed them. "I must ask you to please appreciate that I am here at Laurel Manor to aid in the war effort, and not as a pianist. You understand?"

Iris nodded enthusiastically, a mischievous twinkle in her eye. "I love a good secret, Mr. Van der Hoosen. Don't you worry about that even for a moment. We won't let on that we know who you are, will we, girls?" All four of her daughters murmured their agreement. "Therefore, if you wish to hide your identity from Emma, then I'd suggest you start playing before she returns."

Andrej opened his mouth to object but instead he swallowed his protest. Mrs. Morrison was right. Overly familiar, a tad too forceful, but definitely right.

He closed his eyes and gently placed his hands on the keys before him. The familiar sensation of moving his fingers to match the music in his heart comforted him, as it never failed to do, and he felt the tension leave his body. A life time of seeking, and finding, refuge in his music had been the one true constant in his life.

When he reached the end of the piece, he sat back and looked at his small audience. The tears in Iris' eyes startled him. He found her obvious appreciation of his music touching.

"May we clap now, Mum?" one of the children asked.

Iris nodded. "Yes, of course, love. That's the best way to say thank you to the Maestro for such a lovely gift."

The little girls clapped enthusiastically. Andrej had to clear his throat before speaking, not trusting that his voice wouldn't betray his emotions. He'd never before fully appreciated the difference between playing for a small eager audience versus a faceless crowd of hundreds.

The doors behind him opened and he turned round. Emma was back. His eyes quickly searched her face to see how much she'd overheard.

"It seems I've missed something." She smiled at the small group but Andrej noticed that her eyes went straight to Patrick. He watched as she went over to Iris and reached out for her son, a look of obvious delight playing across her face.

An intense sadness welled up in Andrej's chest. Emma's maternal devotion to Patrick was a wonder to behold. Had his mother ever looked at him with the same joy? He doubted it. What mother delighted in her child and then abandoned him?

Emma, with Patrick cradled in her arms, sat down on the bench beside him. She smiled up at him, a teasing look in her eyes. "Do you take requests?"

Iris saved him from answering by inserting herself into the conversation. "The poor man is going to need a good deal of practice before he's ready to perform, I assure you, Emma." Iris winked at him and simultaneously clapped her hand over her youngest daughter's mouth lest she protest. "Isn't that so, love?" Once the little girl nodded her agreement, Iris dropped her hand.

Stuart stuck his head in the door. "Emma, your delivery is here. Where shall I have the lads set it up?"

Andrej twisted around. Set what up? He'd been so distracted by the visitors that he'd forgotten about Emma's delivery.

"Wonderful, Stuart. Thank you for letting me know. Can you please ask them to bring it in? Better yet, I'll come through." Emma stood, shifting Patrick from the crook of her arm to her shoulder.

"Mr. Van der Hoosen, why don't you hold the baby for Emma?" Iris asked. "It's only for a moment, surely you don't mind?"

Mind? Of course, he minded. He still wasn't used to the sight of an infant, and now she wanted him to actually touch one? "I'm afraid I don't know how," he protested.

"There's honestly not much to it," Iris grinned. She motioned for Emma to hand the baby over to Andrej. "I'd suggest you stay sitting down, Mr. Van der Hoosen. Less of a distance for the baby to fall that way should you drop him." Iris didn't even try to hide her amusement.

He shot her a frown.

"Are you coming, Emma?" Stuart stepped further into the room. "I'll hold the baby. I'm not afraid."

Andrej waved him away. "I've got this, Tollison." He looked to Emma. "I'm ready."

Iris laughed aloud. "Well, hold your arms out, my good man."

Emma gently settled Patrick into the crook of Andrej's left arm. "You simply keep your other arm here," she reached for his right hand and guided it to encircle the baby. "That's all there is to it. Just hold onto him as if he's the most precious thing on earth."

Andrej held his breath as Emma guided the removers, and the enormous crate between them, through to the small room they'd been shown earlier. Stuart hovered close to Emma, which Andrej realized was most likely going to be the young man's habit from now on. He couldn't honestly blame the lad for finding Emma attractive. She was beautiful. And so alive, so warm, how could anyone resist wanting to be near her?

Andrej summonsed a modicum of courage and glanced down at the baby in his arms. Patrick stared up at him with wide, intent eyes. Could babies see well at this age? He honestly had no idea. He stared back, studying each delicate feature. He marveled at the perfectly shaped face, so tiny and yet so exactly proportioned. He reached down and stroked the baby's face with his thumb the way he's seen Emma do. Amazingly, the baby's skin felt even softer than it looked.

He jumped as the glass doors banged open and Lily and Peter came in through them. They were dressed in their school uniforms, both with their book satchels still over their shoulders. They came to stand in front of Andrej. He struggled to think of something to say to them but that was more difficult than he'd have imagined. "How did you find school?" he finally managed.

Lily smiled. "Brilliant. It's so much smaller than our school in London. And the work is easier too, I think."

He glanced at Peter. It was unlike the boy to be so silent. Perhaps his day hadn't been quite as successful as Lily's. The first days at a new school rarely were easy. When it was clear that Peter wasn't going to answer, Andrej introduced the children to Iris. To his immense relief, she guided them over to meet her daughters.

A moment later he felt a tug on his sleeve. Peter had returned.

"We've got a problem, Mr. Van der Hoosen."

Andrej couldn't remember the last time he'd been involved in so many conversations that began with the word 'we'. He wasn't sure he was ready to be confided in.

"What is it, Peter? Don't you like your new school?"

"It's fine."

"Is Lily bothering you?"

"No more than usual."

"Are you ill?"

"Not at all."

"What is this problem then?" Andrej asked.

"It's the baby." Peter looked around to ensure he wouldn't be overheard. He nodded at Patrick. "I think Aunt Emma kidnapped him."

CHAPTER 7

"*H*e didn't believe a word I said." Peter flopped down on his bed and looked at his sister.

"It is a bit much to believe, Peter."

He sighed. He should have known better than to say anything to anyone. But this was important. "I know what I heard."

Lily sat down next to him, her manner sympathetic. "Tell me again just what you think you heard Aunt Emma say."

"I heard her tell Patrick that he was the most well-loved little boy in the world because both she and his mother loved him with all of their hearts."

"Do you think she could have said 'Grandmother' and you didn't hear properly?" Lily asked. "After all you were up in a tree."

Peter shook his head resolutely.

"Perhaps she said 'father' and it just sounded like 'mother,'" Lily tried again.

"But Patrick doesn't have a father," he protested.

"Everyone has a father, Peter."

They sat in silence for a long moment. Peter stole a glance at his sister. She didn't believe him, he knew, but at least she was willing to discuss this with him, which was more than he could say for Mr. Van der Hoosen. He had just looked at Peter with a rather startled expression. Peter wanted to explain the conversation he overhead but, before he'd had a chance, Aunt Emma had come back to take Patrick. Then she had asked them all sorts of questions about their first day of school. He'd kept his answers brief, hoping that he could resume his conversation with Mr. Van der Hoosen but that hadn't worked out.

Once Mr. Van der Hoosen had seen what Aunt Emma had the removers set up in the little room, that had been the end of his chance. He really couldn't understand what all the fuss was about, but Mr. Van der Hoosen had turned to ice and Aunt Emma to fire. Before he even had a chance to witness the blow up that was obviously coming, Iris had whisked them out of ear shot.

"Do you think we should speak to Aunt Joanna about this?" Lily's voice brought him back to the present moment.

Peter considered this for a moment and then shook his head. "What if it causes trouble somehow between Aunt Emma and Aunt Joanna?"

Lily nodded. They both knew that causing trouble between the adults would only lead to problems for themselves. They'd promised their mum they'd not be any trouble. And they liked it at Laurel Cottage. So doing anything, or saying anything, that would perhaps make them have to leave was a bad idea indeed.

"I don't want to be sent away from here," Lily said.

"Neither do I," Peter concurred.

"Will you talk to Mr. Van der Hoosen again do you think?"

Peter shook his head. "If he asks then I will but I doubt he will. He seems to want to stay out of everything, doesn't he?" He turned to look at his sister. "Do you think we make him nervous?"

Lily nodded. "I think we do. I can't imagine why though." She shrugged. "Perhaps he's from a world without children."

Peter's eyes widened. "There's such a place?"

"Yes, I've heard Granny talk about how quiet it must be there."

Peter considered this. Sometimes adults made no sense at all. "I think perhaps we're best off finding out on our own."

"Peter, please don't tell me you mean to snoop on Aunt Emma."

"Snoop?" Peter knew he needed Lily's help, and putting her off wasn't going to help him. What could he say to both reassure her and enlist her help? He smiled as the perfect solution occurred to him. Of course.

"Don't fret, Lily. I won't snoop on anyone." He smiled, feeling suddenly much better. "I know you like Aunt Emma very much. I do too. But tell me what you think of Mr. Van der Hoosen?"

"Oh, I like him well enough I suppose. He's awfully quiet though." Suspicion dawned in her eyes. "What does he have to do with any of this?"

"Nothing, except for the fact that he's single." He strove to keep the excitement out of his voice. He didn't want to alert Lily that he had a plan. Better to let her think she had a part in coming up with the idea. "Aunt Emma is unmarried. And little Patrick doesn't have a father."

"According to you, Peter, he doesn't have a mother either."

He ignored this. "Perhaps there is a logical explanation, Lily, and I just can't see it. Aunt Emma is far more likely to tell an adult about it than she is to tell us."

His sister's nod was encouraging. He was proud of himself for finding a way to rope an unwitting Lily in to his plans. Too often it worked the other way.

"I was thinking that perhaps, just perhaps, we could see if Aunt Emma and Mr. Van der Hoosen could learn to fancy each other." He held his breath, hoping Lily would take the bait.

She did.

"Oh, Peter! You're a brilliant boy!" Lily clapped her hands together. "Yes, if they did then perhaps they could become engaged. Married. They'd be a family for little Patrick." She jumped off the bed and hugged her brother. "You can be clever when you just try."

Peter let that last remark go. She'd called him brilliant and he'd enlisted her help. That was enough for him. He couldn't help but smile. Girls. It was all hearts and flowers to them, wasn't it?

"Wait. What about the baby not belonging to Aunt Emma?" Lily frowned at him. "That's a problem, isn't it?"

Peter knew that to get to the truth he'd need Lily's help. Which meant he'd have to swallow his pride this once. "I suppose I heard wrong like you said, Lily." He shrugged his shoulders. "What really matters is that we help them see what a lovely family they'd make."

His sister's dreamy expression was all the confirmation he needed to know that she was on board.

"What do we do first?" Lily asked. "You do have a plan, don't you?"

"Not yet," Peter lied. "But I'll put some thought into it. Come on, let's go see if it's time for tea." He led the way to the door. He'd think of something, and fast. After all, how hard could it be to get two adults to fall in love?

NAZIS WERE RAVAGING EUROPE, THE WORLD WAS SLOWLY TUMBLING into all-out war and, blast it all, Andrej couldn't even manage to keep his mind off of the woman sitting three feet away. He tossed aside a topographical map of Estonia. He'd been attempting to translate the map key but concentrating was proving impossible. He reached for another from the stack beside him. Perhaps Russia would be intriguing enough to grant him a temporary reprieve from thoughts of Emma.

Cyrillic characters floated before his weary eyes. Names of rivers, towns, and mountains all ran together. It was no use. He took off his reading glasses and rubbed his eyes.

"Why don't you take a break?" Emma asked. She came to stand beside him and Andrej tried not to flinch as she gently rested a hand on his shoulder. Her warmth, always ready in her eyes and her smile, also came through in her touch. He couldn't remember the last time he had so welcomed physical contact with another person. At the same time, he knew it was dangerous to grow accustomed to it. Like the war, like the work at hand, his time with Emma wouldn't last forever.

Emma leaned over his shoulder to see the map in front of him. He moved aside to allow her a better look.

"The Cyrillic alphabet is a mystery to me." Emma sat on the edge of his desk and studied the map. "I wish I could be of more help with these."

Andrej tried to keep his eyes off of Emma's legs. She seemed oblivious to their physical proximity, which clearly meant that she wasn't affected the way he was. The thought made him feel none the better. "It seems there's no end to the work."

"Oh, it's not all that bad, is it?" Emma waved her hand at the stack of maps on the far table. He'd translated them, she'd typed up his notes, and their work was done for the night. "Look at all we've accomplished in a few short weeks."

Andrej glanced at the wooden clock over the mantle place. It was well after ten o'clock. They'd fallen into the habit of working for several hours each evening after Emma had seen to Peter and Lily's homework and baths. She often brought a plate of food up to the Manor for him and they'd settle in for a companionable few hours of work.

He stood. "Forgive me, Emma. I had no idea it was so late."

"I don't mind working at night." She glanced over at Patrick's cot and smiled. "So long as Patrick is welcome here, I'll stay as long as I'm needed."

Patrick. The baby was the center of Emma's world. From the moment Andrej surrendered his objection to having the baby constantly with them, Emma proved to be a dream to work with. As a secretary, she was beyond capable. Her keen intelligence soon impressed him and her steady good cheer brightened his days.

Her unending source of energy amazed him. She handled Patrick's needs without compromising her work performance. She saw to Peter and Lily with great care, and doubtless she was a great help to Joanna around the cottage. Even Lieutenant Tollison's constant interruptions didn't seem to faze her. But the lad was about to drive Andrej round the bend with his transparent excuses for hanging around Emma.

Peter's claim played again in Andrej's mind. For close to three weeks now he'd done his best to limit his time with Peter and Lily, no easy task that. Avoiding the children was one thing though, forgetting Peter's words was quite another.

Andrej had watched Emma closely to see if anything was truly amiss as Peter claimed. He'd witnessed Emma's obvious joy in Patrick, and the gentleness with which she cradled him whenever she could.

Her fiercely protective nature was everything that a mother's should be. Wasn't it? The easiest course of action would be to forget what Peter had said. But then he remembered the concern in the boy's eyes. Peter's claims may not based in truth but his concerns were real enough.

Andrej remembered only too well being that young, that worried, and not having an adult that he could ask questions of. At first he'd wanted to know when his mother was coming back for him. As the months turned into a year he began to wonder if she was coming back at all. He never asked again. She never did return.

Hell. There was nothing for it but to get to the bottom of it, one way or the other. Either he would be able to put the boy's mind at ease, or heaven forbid, it was true, Andrej would need to find a way to help Emma out of the trouble she was in. Kidnapping was serious business. The thought of Emma in the dock made his stomach turn.

Andrej joined her by the cot, where she stood watching Patrick sleep.

"He sleeps like an angel." She leaned over and gently pulled his blanket up under his tiny chin. She smiled up at Andrej but her smile rapidly faded. "What's wrong, Andrej?"

"Are you happy here, Emma?"

They weren't the words his mind planned to say, but it was the question his heart most wanted answered.

Emma continued looking at him wordlessly for a long moment. She laid a hand on his arm. "I am, more than you could imagine."

Her voice was soft and gentle, for all the world the loveliest sound he'd ever heard. She took a tentative step closer to him, and he reached out to draw her into his arms. With her head against his chest, Andrej felt her relax into his embrace. He wished this moment could last forever.

"Are you?" she asked. "Happy, I mean?"

Andrej closed his eyes and tightened his hold on her. He felt her arms respond in kind, and he laid his cheek against her hair. Lavender. The scent would forever remind him of this precious moment in time.

"I don't know what this feeling is," he said. "I've never felt that I've belonged anywhere, with anyone." Images of Joanna, Will, the children, and Emma played before him, from their laughter at the supper table to the quiet evenings they spent in front of the radio listening to broadcasts from London. He wanted to capture the warmth of these days so that he could create memories that would be something to savor in the cold, lonely days ahead.

Emma drew back and looked up at him. "What about your family?"

"I don't have one." Unbidden, he confessed his truth.

Andrej watched as Emma reached a hand up to trace his jaw with her fingertips. Her gentle exploration of his face felt as if she were examining his soul. Her fingers lingered briefly below his lips, leaving him aching for more of her. For all of her.

"You're not alone now, Andrej." Her voice was quiet, her words almost whispered. "Maybe this feeling you can't name means you belong here with us."

Belong. With us. Andrej savored the unfamiliar words.

He looked deep into Emma's eyes, marveling at the openness, the tenderness, he found there. With a gentleness that belied the growing passion building between them, Andrej drew Emma closer still.

He lowered his mouth to hers in a tentative kiss, delighting in her apparent willingness. Nothing could have prepared him for the thrill he felt as she reached her arms up around his neck. Her lips soon parted for him and Andrej felt himself dangerously close to an endless abyss of physical desire and emotional vulnerability.

As Emma moaned softly, Andrej tore his lips from hers and blazed a trail of kisses along her neck. When she tightened her hold on him, he knew she was losing herself to the same passion that was threatening to consume him. His lips hovered at the base of her throat and he smiled when she called out his name, her voice low and husky.

"Sweet, sweet Emma," he whispered against the softness of her skin. His mouth found hers once again. Never had he held such perfection, tasted such sweetness, and he wanted the moment to last forever.

A loud knock on the outer door startled them both and Andrej immediately drew back, the swiftness of his movement causing her to gasp.

"Emma, are you still in there?" Flight Lieutenant Tollison's voice called out.

Andrej had thus far been tolerant of the young man's obvious affection for Emma but now he cursed the airman under his breath.

Startled from his slumber, Patrick let out a demanding wail. Andrej stepped farther away from Emma, from the baby, from the connection with her that had been all too sweet, all too brief.

Stuart's knocking grew persistently louder. "Emma, are you in there? I hear the baby."

"Wait, Stuart," she called out. "Let me put out the light." She quickly switched off the lamp on Andrej's desk and called for him to enter.

As the door closed behind him, she switched the lamp back on. They couldn't take the chance of even a sliver of light escaping into the outer room with it's large windows. The Germans were growing increasingly aggressive with their nighttime bombing raids.

"Stuart, what on earth are you doing here so late?" Emma asked.

Andrej watched as the younger man approached Emma. A bitterness that he refused to name rose in his throat.

"I rang the cottage and Mr. Metcalf said that you were still working. I thought I'd see you and the baby safely home. Are you about ready to leave?" He followed Emma's gaze to where Andrej stood in the shadows. "Oh, good evening, Sir. I didn't see you lurking there."

Lurking. For a single shilling he'd throttle the lad. Fresh-faced and eager, Tollison was clearly and completely infatuated. But Andrej could hardly blame the young airman for being captivated by Emma. He himself was.

"Good evening, Lieutenant Tollison." Andrej stepped out of the darkness. "It's good of you to take such thoughtful care of Miss Bradley."

Emma had gathered Patrick up, his cries subsiding as she rocked him. "We're not quite done here, Stuart." She looked pointedly at Andrej.

"It's too late, Emma." He meant more than the hour and she knew it.

"Andrej, please--"

"Did I interrupt something important?" Stuart asked, glancing between the two. "I don't mind waiting while you finish up."

"No." Andrej shook his head. He carefully avoided Emma's gaze. The last thing he wanted to see was regret or pity in her eyes. "We're done."

Stuart took Emma's jacket off the coat tree and slipped it over her shoulders. For the world to see, they looked the perfect picture of a young, happy couple.

"There'll be plenty of work tomorrow first thing," Stuart said. "Word is that the Italians are edging toward Greece. Wing Commander Blythe said he would be by in the morning to brief you on which Greek islands they'd like you to look at first."

"Certainly," Andrej nodded. He sat down at his desk and pulled a map of Latvia toward him. "I'll be here waiting for him in the morning."

"Won't you head back to Laurel Cottage with us?" Stuart asked.

Andrej shook his head. He was right where he belonged, on the outside of 'us'. He focused his attention on the task at hand. "No, go on ahead. I much prefer the solitude here," he said without looking up.

"Good night, Andrej," Emma said, her voice tentative, unsure.

He lifted his hand in lieu of an answer. He couldn't trust his voice not to betray the emotions he wanted to keep to himself.

He switched off the lamp and waited until the door closed behind them before turning it on again. The light was easily brought back with a simple flick of his fingers. His peace of mind wasn't so easily restored.

～

"Can you see anything, Peter?"

"Not unless you get out of the way."

"Sorry." Lily moved back and settled for looking over Peter's shoulder. "It would be ever so much easier if we had a torch light. I can hardly see anything in all this darkness."

"You can blame the Germans for that. When the war is over I think I shall keep the light on all night long if I please." Peter leaned his forehead against their bedroom window pane. "Wait. I think I see a shadow. Oh, yes, it's them."

"They're back late. That's a good sign."

"Don't get too excited." Peter groaned. "It's Aunt Emma and Patrick alright but they're not with Mr. Van der Hoosen. They're with that fellow. Again."

Lily scampered back under her bed covers and pulled them up under her chin. "I give up."

Peter took himself off to his bed. Dejection wasn't his normal reaction when thwarted, but really, this match-making business was far more difficult than he'd first thought. The way Lieutenant Tollison constantly hovered around Emma was outside of enough.

"There are two problems with giving up, Lily." Peter flipped over onto his side and propped his head up on his elbow. He waited for his sister to the do the same so he was sure she was in the mood to conference. Once she did, he continued. "First of all, what else are we meant to do with ourselves until it's time to go home? Worry about Mum and Granny every moment of the day?"

"Don't forget Daddy."

Peter swallowed the lump in his throat which instantly appeared whenever he thought of his father. "And Daddy, you're right. Worrying about Aunt Emma and Mr. Van der Hoosen learning to fancy each other is so much easier, don't you think?"

"Absolutely," she agreed. "What's the other reason we shouldn't give up?"

"Patrick." Peter considered his words carefully. Lily still thought he had heard Aunt Emma wrong but he knew better. At first, he'd been worried about Patrick's real mother missing her baby. Now he realized that he was far more worried about what would happen to Aunt Emma if she were found out. At the very least, she'd go to jail. He hated the idea because he'd grown quite fond of her. It almost felt like she was his real aunt. He and Lily owed it to her to help her out of the trouble she was in.

"When we go back home to be with Mum and Dad I worry about what's going to happen to little Patrick," Peter told his sister. "He should have a father. I think Mr. Van der Hoosen could learn how to be a proper parent, don't you?"

Lily considered the question. "I suppose so. After all, he's learned how to hold Patrick sometimes when Aunt Emma asks him to. He's looking less nervous each time."

"I think he's got definite potential," Peter agreed. He was quiet a moment, cocking his head toward the open door. "Shhh ...Aunt Emma's coming. Pretend you're asleep."

Peter lay still when Emma came in to straighten their duvets. Lily's pretend snores were definitely overkill. He made a mental note to mention that to her later. He waited a full five minutes after Emma was gone to call to his sister. "Lily, are you awake?"

"Of course, I'm still awake, Peter."

"Those snores sounded so real, I wasn't sure." He'd learned during the last few weeks that a little praise went a very long way with his sister. "Why don't you go and knock on Aunt Emma's door and ask her some girly question. See what you can find out."

Lily padded out of the room but was back in less than a minute.

"She sent you away?" Peter asked, incredulous. That was so unlike Aunt Emma.

"No," Lily shook her head. "I didn't even knock. Oh, Peter, through the door I could hear her sobbing."

"She was crying?"

"No, not crying. Sobbing."

"What's the difference?"

"Sobbing is much sadder than crying." Lily climbed back under the covers. Her voice was grave. "She was definitely sobbing."

CHAPTER 8

"*M*arry me, Emma."

"Go away, won't you, Stuart?"

"At least send me off with a kiss," he tried again, undeterred by the lack of consideration shown to his proposal.

"No deal." Emma took a stack of folders to the bank of cabinets along the back wall of the inner office. "Really, Stuart, isn't there anything else you should be doing?"

"I much prefer to be here with you rather than face the never-ending stack of paperwork coming across my desk." He watched as Emma set about filing, appreciating her trim figure as much as he did her beautiful features. In a house overrun with men, it was a treat to be able to spend time with such a lovely girl. He was a lucky chap.

"You flatter me to no end." Emma bent down and tugged at the bottom cabinet but it wouldn't budge. She gave it a good kick but even that didn't do the trick. "Did you ever stop and think that the work seems never ending because you're not actually doing any of it?"

He got up from the chair beside her desk and crossed to the cabinets. With only a slight tug he pulled the offending drawer open. A grin stretched across his face. He leaned in toward Emma. "I demand a kiss for my efforts, Miss Bradley."

"Would you really demand it of me, Stuart?"

"Of course not," he said, surprised by the seriousness that suddenly entered her voice. "I would never demand anything from you. I like you too much."

His answer restored the smile to Emma's face.

"You're a good lad, Stuart, and right after the war is over I'm going to help you settle down by finding you a nice girl."

"But I don't want a nice girl. I want you."

This won him a laugh. Which made him smile in turn.

"Such flattery, Lieutenant Tollison, I hardly know what to say."

"Say you'll kiss me," he tried again. "At least once, Emma, if for no other reason than to compare me to the last man fortunate enough to kiss you."

To his great surprise, this last desperate bit seemed to do the trick. Emma leaned toward him. "Go ahead, Stuart, prove that the last man I kissed was no different than any other."

He reached out to cup Emma's face in his hands and take her lips to his. He barely was able to show her that he knew what he was about before the office door burst open.

"Emma, I've just reviewed the first of--"

Stuart stepped back guiltily at the sight of Andrej, his arms laden down with maps.

An awkward silence filled the room. Stuart looked apologetically at Emma before he cleared his throat. "Pardon me, Sir, I was disturbing Miss Bradley whilst she was attempting to work."

"Odd, she doesn't look particularly disturbed to me, Lieutenant." Andrej dumped the maps onto Emma's desk. Her phone rang and he picked it up and spoke to the caller. After a moment he motioned for Stuart to come closer.

"It's a call from London for you, Tollison."

Stuart took the receiver and offered his thanks to Andrej's already departing back. He sighed. "Flight Lieutenant Tollison here."

"Stuart, my good fellow, I'm delighted to track you down in my niece's office. Is she there with you?"

His eyes drifted to where Emma had returned to her filing. "Affirmative, Sir."

"Good lad for not letting on it's me. You haven't said anything to her about my being in touch with you?"

"No, Sir, I gave you my word I wouldn't."

"Is Emma's baby with her right now? In the room with her, I mean."

Stuart couldn't help but think that Emma's Uncle Malcolm was an odd man judging by the questions he asked. Still, he apparently cared enough to check in on Emma regularly. Stuart didn't mind taking the man's calls. How could keeping Emma's uncle apprised of her and the baby's welfare be a problem? "That he is, Sir. Usually not ever more than a few feet away."

"Excellent, excellent." There was a silence at the end of the phone for a long moment. "Has Emma said anything to you yet about her baby's father?"

"No, Sir. It hasn't come up and I didn't think it was my place to ask. He must be a right barmy though to leave her in the lurch like this." He realized he'd spoken too freely when Emma threw a sharp glance his way. He'd best mind his tongue.

"There's a bit more to it than that, my boy. But there'll be time enough for details later. Tell me this, you are growing fond of my niece?"

"Tremendously so, Sir."

"Very good. I think you might be just the young man to help me get through to her. No doubt she'll be overwhelmed with emotion when she realizes the part you've played in our reconciliation, but it's imperative that you keep our conversations strictly between us for now. Is that understood?"

Stuart reassured the other man and rang off. He couldn't help but be pleased at the thought of Emma's reaction when she found out that he'd been in contact with her Uncle Malcolm. Favorite uncle, hadn't the man said?

"I'm off, Emma." He smiled at her and waved goodbye. He'd collect his kiss tomorrow, soon enough. "Don't forget you promised to see a film with me Saturday afternoon."

"And you promised that I could bring Patrick, Peter, and Lily," Emma raised an eyebrow at him. "Are you still sure you want to take us all?"

"Is it the only way I'm going to be able to see you?"

Her smile was apologetic. "It is."

"Then I'll see you all at three o'clock. Cheerio."

"HE'S AN ABSOLUTE DISH, ISN'T HE?" IRIS POPPED A BIT OF APPLE INTO her mouth. "God, I wish this were chocolate."

Emma laughed, something she did frequently when she was with Iris. Unexpectedly finding a friend in Iris had helped ease her loneliness. She missed London, she missed her friends, she missed her flat and neighbors, and most of all she missed her cousin Patricia. She sighed.

"What are you sighing so deeply about?" Iris asked. "The lack of chocolate or your dishy man?"

"I don't have a man at all, dishy or not," Emma answered. "I think the lack of sweets is driving you mad."

She leaned over to check on Patrick, fast asleep in the Moses basket beside her chair. Iris had finished nursing him but Emma was reluctant to leave just yet. Peter and Lily were tearing round the garden with Iris' daughters. She felt too content to move.

"By my count, you have two men."

"Unless you're referring to Patrick and Peter, I don't have a clue what you're talking about."

Iris threw back her head and laughed, a sound that drew the children to the window to see what was so funny. She waved them away, still giggling.

"Don't act daft with me, Emma Bradley. You know full well that I'm referring to that lovesick young lieutenant and your dishy Dutch boss."

"Stuart isn't my young man. He's just a very nice friend, that's all. He's funny and kind and he takes my mind off of other things."

"Other things meaning Andrej Van der Hoosen?"

Andrej was the last person Emma wanted to talk about with anyone, especially Iris. Her friend was too perceptive for Emma's comfort. She didn't want a voice given to her feelings, mixed up as they were.

The fact that she was physically attracted to Andrej was undeniable. She remembered the gentle way his hands had held her close, the softness of his lips against hers. Her passionate response to Andrej hadn't alarmed her in the moment. Yet in the clear light of day, the way she'd surrendered her self-control was frightening. It couldn't happen again.

"I'm going to hazard a guess that the dreamy expression on your face isn't because you're thinking of our young lieutenant?"

Emma frowned. Sometimes Iris seemed just too pleased with herself.

"Let us just get totally carried away and say, for the sake of argument, that I have noticed what a charming, handsome man Andrej is, it doesn't change anything," Emma said. "I'm not interested in any man whatsoever, period, under any circumstances, ever again. Not even a penniless but handsome piano teacher will change my mind."

"What makes you think Andrej is penniless?"

Emma shrugged. "I can't imagine that piano teachers earn very much money."

"Piano teacher?" Iris grinned. "Is that what he told you he does for a living?"

"He hasn't told me anything about his life in London."

"But you've asked, haven't you, and that tells me something."

Emma rolled her eyes. She didn't try to hide her exasperation. "I ask questions of everyone. It's a bad habit of mine."

"You've never asked me what I was doing before the war."

"Iris, you have five children under the age of ten years old. I know what you were doing before the war."

"Touché," Iris laughed good-naturedly. "If you don't want to talk about Andrej I'll let it go…for now." She shifted round in her chair to better face Emma, her expression suddenly serious. "Tell me about Patrick's father then. Is there any chance of reconciliation? Some sort of misunderstanding that could be cleared up?"

Emma shook her head resolutely. "Not a chance, Iris. There's more likelihood that Herr Hitler will become the next Pope."

Iris wrinkled her nose. "Vile image."

"Vile, that's just what Malcolm is…he's loathsome and I detest him." Emma could feel the heat of her hatred burn through her. "I'd sooner run over him with your husband's lorry than look at him again."

"Malcolm, is it?"

Emma winced. Anger had loosened her tongue for the first and last time, she vowed. She had to be more careful.

"Emma, you must know that you're going to have to answer questions someday. Perhaps not my questions but plenty of people are going to wonder. Patrick is going to want to know what kind of man his father is."

"He's violent, Iris. He's a dangerous, lying bastard, and I need you to promise you won't ask me again," she implored. "Promise me."

Iris reached over and hugged Emma. "Did he hurt you?"

The memory of Patricia's lifeless body at the bottom of the staircase made her heart both ache and rage at the same time. "His violence knows no limits." Her voice caught in her throat. "I wouldn't trust him alone with Patrick, his own flesh and blood, for the time it would take me to blink."

Iris patted her hand reassuringly. "I swear I won't ever ask again. In fact, I'll lie to the devil himself if it would help protect you and the baby."

The devil himself. Emma shuddered.

"I CAN'T SAY AS I EVER REMEMBER TASTING ONE," PETER SAID. "Although I must have done before the war started, I'd imagine."

Andrej couldn't help but smile at the way Peter was so carefully examining the orange. The boy had joined him in the sitting room as he'd opened the package, a gift from an opera singer in Florida that he had worked with years ago. Lily was working on her sums at the kitchen table, which was where Peter was meant to be. However, curiosity about a package from America had been too much for the boy to resist. Andrej reached into the box before him and pulled out another orange.

"There are more here, Peter, so go ahead and eat that one now."

"I'll wait for Lily and split it with her."

Andrej reached over and ruffled the boy's hair. "Good lad, but there's enough for you to have one and there will be more for you both later. It's kind of you to share."

"Don't think I haven't noticed you sharing your extra food with me," Peter replied. "I know you're being nice but you needn't worry I'm going to starve just because I am sometimes hungry."

"Growing lads shouldn't go hungry."

"Were you hungry when you were growing up?"

Andrej was quiet for a moment. He'd never been hungry. Neither had he ever been cold. His physical needs, at least, had always been met. "There was a war on when I was just a bit older than Lily is now, but Holland was neutral." The confused look on Peter's face led him to add, "The Dutch didn't take one side or the other. They watched from the sidelines."

"Oh, you mean like the Irish are doing now?" Peter gave a low whistle. "You should hear what my granny says about that." He peeled an orange and handed a portion to Andrej. He popped a slice into his mouth and made a face. "Sour, sweet, and delicious, Lily is going to love this. So, is that where you learned to stand aside and just watch everyone?"

Andrej's eyebrows rose. "I don't know what you're talking about."

"Certainly you do, Sir. You're quiet during dinner. Whenever we're all together, you listen carefully to everything everyone says, and yet you never tell us what you're thinking."

"I suppose I'm not used to anyone caring one way or the other about what I think." Andrej was startled by the honesty in his reply. He'd never put the sentiment into words, but then again, no one had ever questioned him the way Peter was now. "Is there something specific that you wished to know?"

Peter nodded. "Tell me what you think of Aunt Emma."

Andrej's eyes widened. How on earth to answer this?

"Do you like her?"

"Like her?" Andrej repeated.

"Fancy her," Peter repeated the words slowly, as if talking to a young child. "Do you fancy Aunt Emma?"

Andrej opened his mouth to answer but closed it just as quickly. How to put his feelings for Emma into words? Her beauty enchanted him, her wit amused him, her kindness touched him, yet he knew these feelings endangered his heart.

Peter eyed him expectantly.

"What do you think of her?" Andrej volleyed the question back to Peter.

"Oh, we think she's grand. Flat out fun but sort of motherly at the same time. But I asked you first."

Andrej took a deep breath. The whole concept of talking about his emotions was new to him, but perhaps Peter was a safe place to practice doing so. "I think Emma is the most remarkable woman I've ever met."

Peter nodded expectantly, encouraging him to say more.

Why not? It wasn't as if he were talking to Emma. "She's beautiful beyond words, isn't she? Skin so smooth and soft, and her eyes, Peter, they hold such warmth and compassion. When I'm in the same room with her my heart feels so full."

"So, you're saying she's quite the looker, aren't you?" Peter grinned.

Andrej shook his head in mock disapproval but a smile pulled at his lips. "Yes, she is, Peter, but that's not how we properly refer to women, is it?"

"That's your first 'we' sentence since I've known you, Mr. Van der Hoosen." Peter grinned. "Lily will be quite chuffed to hear it. Bravo!"

Andrej realized he was in over his head with Peter. The lad was far too observant for his comfort. "Now, Peter, what I've just said is between you and I alone. It's not something I want you repeating to Emma."

Peter shrugged, his smile satisfied. "I won't have to. Aunt Emma's just behind you."

Andrej silently cursed his loose tongue and turned slowly around. True to Peter's word, Emma stood leaning in the doorway.

She was the first to break the awkward silence. "Peter, aren't you meant to be doing your sums?"

The boy slid off the arm of the chair, a frown creasing his forehead. "I don't know why I bother. It seems we'd be better off studying German. That way, when the Jerrys invade, we'll be able to tell them how much we hate them in their own language."

Emma caught him by the shoulders as he tried to walk past her. She bent down and looked him straight in the eye. "An invasion isn't inevitable, Peter. There are too many brave people here in Britain working hard day and night to make sure that won't happen."

"You can't promise me they won't find a way."

"No, you're right, I can't." Emma looked to Andrej and he came to stand beside them, his earlier embarrassment gone in the wake of Peter's concern. He knelt down beside Emma and squeezed Peter's arm reassuringly.

"You'd best trust Emma on this Peter." Andrej looked into Peter's eyes. The lad's natural mischievousness had been edged aside with worry. The boy's stark vulnerability saddened him. "I cannot imagine there are Germans brave enough, strong enough, or even foolish enough to think they can invade England and live to tell about it. If you ever decide to study the German language, let it be from a place of peace and not anger, yes?"

"You speak German, don't you, Sir?"

"Fluently."

"Then perhaps you can tell them we don't want them here if they do come."

Andrej nodded. "I shall tell them for all of us in the unlikely event it comes to that."

Peter flung himself at Andrej and Emma, his arms encircling them both. Andrej quickly put an arm around Emma to avoid her being knocked off balance by the boy's impetuous embrace. He gingerly patted Peter on the back, unsure how best to offer comfort.

"Off you go, Peter," Emma said. "Nazis or not, you've got your sums to finish."

Andrej stood and helped Emma to her feet as Peter left the room, banging the door closed behind him. He made to move away but she laid a hand on his arm.

"Thank you, Andrej, for reassuring him." She smiled up at him.

Her smile went straight to his heart, the way it always did. He took a step back from her and looked away. "His fears are understandable."

They were both silent for a long moment. As much as he wished otherwise, there was nothing for it but to try to explain away what she'd overheard when she'd come looking for Peter.

"Emma, I apologize for what you overheard. I meant no disrespect." As apologies went, Andrej knew his was woefully inadequate.

"I don't know that I've been called a 'looker' before," Emma said, enough amusement in her voice that Andrej felt compelled to meet her eye. "There's no call to apologize."

Andrej knew he should leave the room to avoid the desire that was yet again threatening his sanity. Truth told though, he didn't want to resist. Emma was only a few feet away, looking up at him. Surely she knew better than to trust him after his deplorable lack of control the other evening?

"On the contrary, Emma, I think I have a great deal to apologize for." Andrej sat on the arm of the sofa and crossed his arms over his chest, as if to ward off her charms.

"For what, Andrej? Kissing me?" She now stood squarely in front of him, the desire in her eyes clear and unapologetic. "I didn't complain. Don't you remember?"

Remember? He'd thought of little else but how she'd felt in his arms. He longed to reach out and draw her close her to him now. But he resisted the urge. His growing desire for Emma was a flame he was reluctant to get to close to.

Emma reached out a tentative hand and traced an invisible pattern along his arm, the lightness of her touch searing his skin. His eyes left hers only to memorize the fullness of her lips.

He caught her hand and raised it to his lips. Unable, no, unwilling, to stop himself, he drew her into his arms. "Emma, tell me to stop," his voice was barely above a whisper.

Her answer was to reach up and thread her fingers through his hair. He shivered at the intimacy of her touch, her obvious invitation, and he gently took possession of her lips in a kiss shamelessly meant to steal her warmth, her softness, and keep it all for himself.

After an endless moment Emma pulled back. Concerned, Andrej searched her eyes. Had he frightened her? Had he hurt her? He'd sooner die.

Emma put a finger against his lips. "You needn't hold me as if you are afraid to crush me, you know." She smiled at him with no hint of reservation.

Andrej closed his eyes and groaned as Emma reached up to brush her lips against his ear, the warmness of her breath no match for the heat of his desire. She softly, slowly, with excruciating deliberateness, kissed him along his jaw and neck, nearly driving him mad with longing. He tightened his hold on her as her fingers search for his shirt buttons.

She unfastened the first, then second button, and slid her hand in, flat against his chest. Doubtless she felt his heart racing but he was beyond caring. She knew the passion her touch was eliciting, and the exploration of her hands told him she wasn't afraid of his response.

He moved to sit on the couch and he pulled Emma down on his lap. Her breathless gasp was not a protest, though, and Andrej was determined to touch her, delight her, the way she had him. He slid his hand behind the nape of her neck and pulled her mouth to his. With his other hand, following her lead, he traced his fingers along her neckline and downward until he found a button standing between his fingers and the delicate swell of her breasts.

A knock on the door broke through their passion. "Aunt Emma, may I come in?"

It was Lily. Andrej didn't know whether he should curse or be grateful for the interruptions that plagued them.

"Just a moment, Lily. I'll be right there." Emma's voice sounded amazingly level, but the unevenness of her breathing as she hastily smoothed her hair belied her passionate response to his touch.

Andrej got to his feet. He looked down in surprise when Emma squeezed his arm.

"Don't you dare tell me again that you're sorry, Andrej," Emma whispered before she crossed to the door and pulled it open.

"I apologize for disturbing you, Aunt Emma." Lily peered in the room and waved to Andrej.

He waved back. To his amazement, Lily seemed blissfully unaware that she'd interrupted anything.

"A phone call from London came for you," Lily said.

"Are they holding the line now?"

Lily shook her head. "No, but the man asked me to give you a message. He said to tell you that he thinks of you and Patrick often."

Andrej watched in surprise as Emma took a step back from Lily as if she'd been struck.

"He also said that he hoped you were both comfortable here. And he said that he thought of his baby's mother often."

"He said it just like that?" Emma's words were sharp.

"Yes, those were his exact words." Lily shifted uncomfortably from one foot to the other. "That was all he said. Are you all right, Aunt Emma?"

Emma's only answer was to choke back a sob as she buried her face in her hands.

Andrej came to stand beside Lily. "You're a good girl, my dear, to remember that message. You go finish your sums and I'll stay with Emma."

Lily smiled gratefully at him and slipped out of the room, shutting the door carefully behind her. Andrej waited until she was gone before he spoke. "Emma? What's this about?"

When she turned to him, the alarm in her eyes stunned him. He reached out to comfort her but she cowered from his touch as if she feared he'd strike her. She took a few steps backward, fumbled with the door handle, and slipped out of the room.

Andrej stood and stared at the door long after Emma left the room. What on earth had her so frightened? He frowned as he remembered Peter's comment about Emma not being Patrick's real mother. Was this proof that the boy was on to something?

CHAPTER 9

*E*mma found the next month at Laurel Cottage to be one of endless agony. Worry, grief and loneliness hounded her when she wasn't working or busy with the children. She peered out of her bedroom window but was unable to see anything for the rain that pelted against the glass panes in a relentless assault on her remaining sanity.

She sat at her dressing table where she'd earlier been attempting to write a cheerful, uplifting letter to her parents in Canada. Censoring each word so that her mother and father wouldn't worry about her any more than strictly necessary was draining. She missed them terribly. Trying to make her time at Laurel Cottage sound idyllic was impossible because her parents listened to the same broadcasts from London that she did. The Germans were attempting to bomb the very life out of London, night after night without fail. The southern coastal areas weren't exempt from nighttime bombing raids either and her parents were astute enough to realize this.

Patrick sighed in his sleep and Emma peeked into his cot to check that he was warm enough. Babies, children, and worry were a package deal. Isn't that what her mother used to say when she was a child? It hadn't meant anything then but now she understood. Her parents knew she had Patrick with her but they thought Patricia's death the result of a tragic accident. She scribbled a few details on how rapidly the baby was growing and what a joy he was, at least that part was true. If the road to hell was paved with lies, she must be at least half way there by now. At this point, how much did one more lie matter?

As soon as we're able, Patrick and I will join you in Canada, until then don't worry about us. Love always, Emma

Canada. Emma sighed as she neatly folded her letter and slipped it into an envelope. She'd not wanted to leave England before the war, and no more did she now. Malcolm wasn't in Canada though, and that made it the perfect place to travel to as soon as they could book safe passage. But when? Months from now? Years from now? Surely the war couldn't go on much longer?

The constant uncertainty of what she should do gave Emma a headache. She rubbed her temples but that didn't help. A cup of tea sounded heavenly, but she didn't want to go downstairs until she was certain that Iris was gone. But the incessant rain meant that her friend most likely hadn't left the cottage yet.

Perhaps she should feel guilty for being so uncharitable but she was still cross with Iris. She didn't feel like being subjected to her friend's relentless matchmaking efforts again today. True to her word, Iris hadn't ever mentioned Malcolm again. But she did argue that she and Patrick would be safer if Emma was married and had the protection of a husband.

Ironic, Emma thought, that Iris believed the solution to her trouble would end with a man, when that was precisely where it had begun.

Iris had settled on Stuart as the ideal husband. What had she said? "You'll be able to get almost anything by him easily and he'll follow you to Canada without a single objection." Which would be ideal if they were talking about a puppy, but obedience wasn't a quality Emma ever thought to prize in a husband. She replayed in her head the arguments that Iris had made for marriage, but her heart didn't want to accept the idea that it was her only choice.

From the corner of her eye, Emma noticed a folded piece of paper slide under her door. She retrieved it, the smallest of smiles crossing her face, defying her foul mood. Peter and Lily had listened carefully and considerately when she'd asked them not to knock on her door during Patrick's afternoon naps. They'd soon discovered, however, that a piece of paper slid under the door didn't make sufficient noise to wake the baby.

Aunt Emma – FLT LT Tollison rang and said he'll call round at five o'clock to pick you up for tonight's dance – Lily

Emma groaned. The dance at Laurel Manor. She'd forgotten all about it. Obviously, Stuart hadn't. When he'd first asked her to accompany him to the dance it sounded like a welcome break from the monotonous worry that defined her evenings.

She shared supper every evening with Will, Joanna, and the children but Andrej had been conspicuously absent at the cottage during the last few weeks. It was her fault. After Malcolm had rung the cottage and left a message with Lily, Emma had retreated into a mental cave of worry. Andrej had tried on numerous occasions to draw her out but she'd rejected his efforts. Repeatedly.

Now the only time they spoke was at work. Andrej made eye contact only when strictly necessary and he managed to stay on the opposite side of the room as often as possible. She didn't blame him. Obviously, her rejection hurt him but she couldn't make herself confide in him.

Emma gingerly pulled open the wardrobe doors, mindful not to wake the baby. She flipped through the dresses that hung neatly on the rack and summarily dismissed them all. She just wasn't in the mood for festivities of any sort. But if she tried to cry off, everyone would badger her to go out. Stuart would expect a smile on her face. If he didn't see one, he'd work tirelessly to put one there.

Stuart really was nice enough. But even so, Emma couldn't help but think of him as she once had the boy next door who followed her everywhere from the time she was six until she was ten. Stuart was thoughtful. He was kind. He was funny.

He just wasn't Andrej.

Emma closed the wardrobe doors and sat on the edge of her bed.

She missed Andrej. She missed his calm, quiet presence. His rare but ever-so-charming smile. Stop, stop, stop, she chided herself. Her life was complex, confusing and turbulent enough, without delving into her feelings for a man she could never be with.

Another piece of paper slid under the door.

Aunt Emma – I think you'd look smashing in your green dress. Aunt Joanna says she has pearls that you are very welcome to wear tonight. I can't wait to see how lovely you look all dressed up – Lily

Emma smiled. Lily was a darling little girl. She and Peter both were so bravely enduring their forced separation from their mother. If it made Lily happy to see Emma go to the Manor tonight, then she'd go.

She sat in front of the dressing table and frowned at her reflection. How she longed for straight hair instead of her cursed curls that never stayed pinned. It took her just under a quarter hour to straighten and then roll back her hair. Pushing the last pin into place, she saw yet another note slide under the door. Hopefully Stuart had rung up to cancel.

Emma – You can't hide in there forever. Open the door – Iris

Knowing there was nothing for it, Emma opened the door and stood aside as Iris sailed in.

"The children were almost out of paper so I'm glad it only took one written request to gain admittance."

"You're welcome to stay if you can refrain from talking about Stuart," Emma warned her.

"Stuart who?" Iris grinned. She settled on Emma's bed, glancing at the baby's cot. "Patrick sleeps like no other baby I've ever seen."

"He's a blessing." Emma looked down at him for a long moment, her heart so full of love that she had to resist the temptation to scoop him up and cover his tiny face with kisses. "Speaking of which, where are your girls?"

"Downstairs having a German lesson. Can you guess whose idea the impromptu class was?"

"Peter's, naturally."

"Am I allowed to mention the teacher's name or is he also a taboo subject?"

"Andrej's downstairs?" Emma's heartbeat quickened. It was unlike him to be home so early.

"He is." Iris smiled, looking altogether too satisfied with herself for Emma's liking. "I heard him say that he just came by to pick up something he'd forgotten, but Peter roped him into teaching them some German phrases."

"Such as?"

"The first thing Peter thought they should learn was, 'No, you may not sit at the table with us. Eat on the floor with the dogs.'"

For the first time in a month, Emma laughed. "Are you telling me that Andrej's gone along with this?"

"He has a slightly bewildered look on his face," Iris shared. "But yes, he's indulging them. He really is a lovely man."

Emma nodded but didn't trust herself to speak. The last thing she needed was for Iris, however well meaning, to pick up on Emma's feelings for Andrej. He was a just a man she worked with, nothing more.

Liar, her inner voice taunted her. Andrej wasn't just a coworker. He was a man she wanted to spend time with, to talk with, to laugh with. She wanted him to touch her, hold her. She even wished that he was someone she could confide the truth about Patrick to but it could never happen. Never.

Emma had learned to doubt her instincts, for as much as Malcolm was to blame for pushing Patricia down the stairs to her death, she blamed herself as well. When she'd learned that Malcolm and Patricia were seeing each other she'd been alarmed but hadn't demanded Patricia stop seeing him. Instead, she trusted that, given the time, Patricia would see Malcolm for the snake he was.

When she finally did, it was too late. Patricia was pregnant with Malcolm's baby. Even then Emma hadn't understood the depths of cruelty in Malcolm's heart. There was blood on her hands as much as his because she'd looked into the face of evil and hadn't recognized it for exactly what it was.

Patrick's cooing noises broke through Emma's thoughts. She scooped him up and held him close, murmuring endearments to him all the while.

"Patrick's actually the reason I came up here, Emma. Let me take him home with me for the evening so that you can properly enjoy the dance."

Emma resolutely shook her head. "No, that is generous of you but I'm taking him with me."

"Into a loud, smoke-filled room with dozens of airmen slugging back as much lager as they can? There's a winning idea if I've heard one." Iris shook her head. "Let him come home with me. You needn't be frightened. I'll snap Malcolm's head off his shoulders if he shows up."

"It's not funny, Iris." Emma shuddered. She'd not heard from Malcolm since he'd phoned that one time. His silence was unnerving.

"I'm sorry, really I am. But I just wanted to do you a good turn. You've been a smashing friend and having you to visit with has helped me pass the time until Robert comes home."

Emma shot a guilty look at the other woman. Iris was so good-natured and determined to laugh at everything that it was easy for Emma to forget that she had her fair share of loneliness to bear.

"He'll be much better off with me tonight," Iris persisted. "Joanna is going to bring Peter and Lily up to my house for a long visit. Patrick will be warm, well fed, and perfectly safe. I promise."

"You don't want to come to the dance?"

"Whatever for?" Iris pulled a face. "I have a husband already, unlike you...oh, my mistake. I wasn't supposed to use that word, was I?"

Emma rolled her eyes. "You're incorrigible."

"Truthfully, it's Robert's night to ring us from London and I don't want to miss his call. The children play so well together. You can come fetch Patrick first thing tomorrow."

Emma hesitated. She didn't want to go the dance, she didn't want to be away from Patrick for even a few hours, let alone all night. And she didn't want to spend the evening pretending to be happy so that Stuart wouldn't fuss.

What she really wished she could do was crawl into her bed and have a good, long cry. Her self-pity was indulgent. The least she could do was just go along with the plans everyone else was making. Tomorrow would be soon enough to get back to her worries.

"As always, you win. I'll be round to fetch Patrick in the morning." She managed a smile for her friend. "I promise to try to enjoy myself."

"Brilliant. Now get yourself dressed up and I'll wait downstairs with the children." She stopped, her hand on the door. "I'm going to see if Andrej will teach me to say, 'Your mother is ugly' in German." She winked at Emma and was gone.

PETER GENTLY TURNED THE DOOR HANDLE TO AUNT EMMA'S ROOM AND held his breath against hope that the door would not creak. He glanced over his shoulder into the hallway. No one was around. He slipped into the room, closing the door behind him as carefully as he'd opened it. Guilt was a nasty feeling, he decided. What he was doing was wrong. But he was doing it for the right reason.

He looked around. Where to start? If Aunt Emma had a secret, and Peter knew deep in his heart that she did, where would she keep proof of it? He didn't know what he expected to find. Maybe he could find a birth certificate that had Patrick's real parents names on it. Maybe they'd be so happy to get their baby back that they'd be able to forgive her. After all, she'd taken wonderful care of Patrick. Surely, they could be made to understand that she hadn't meant any harm.

At least he was sure of one thing. He'd made the right choice by not telling Lily that he was going to look through Aunt Emma's things for a clue. She would have pitched a fit.

As quietly as he was able, Peter crossed over to the writing table by the window. He looked through the neatly stacked envelopes. There was a letter from her parents in Canada. One from Ireland. Interesting. He slipped the letter out of the envelope and scanned it. Boring. If there was a clue here it was written in sort of gossipy female secret language that he'd never be able to decipher. Interestingly, there was no mention of Patrick though. The writer, a friend of Aunt Emma's, had closed the letter with much fondness but hadn't asked after the baby. Some friend.

The next letter was from his mother. Peter dropped it back on the stack and quickly covered it with another. His mother would be furious if she knew that he was going through Emma's things. Snooping, as his sister would call it. It was all well and good that Lily could take the high road, but what was she going to do when the police finally caught up to Aunt Emma and arrested her for kidnapping?

Cry, that was what she was going to do, and a fat lot of good it would do Aunt Emma as she was taken off to jail. No, far better to help her out before she was caught. And the first step to doing so was to find out who Patrick's parents were.

A quick search of the desk drawers turned up nothing interesting. Peter was loathe to go through the bureau. The thought of all of those girlish garments made him blush. He looked around the room. Wasn't there someplace else he could try next instead?

The wardrobe. Peter pulled open the doors and stood back. Dresses. Two pairs of shoes. A valise. That might be a good hiding place. He lifted it out of the wardrobe and onto the floor. The latches sprung open easily. Empty, just as he'd expected. He ran his hands along the lining and hoped he'd feel a...what did he hope to find? A birth certificate is what he really needed. But there were no packets of papers or anything else in the case. He closed it again and placed it back in the wardrobe.

He was just about to close the doors when he caught sight of a handbag. His heart rate quickened as he snapped it open. Whatever guilt he'd wrestled with before, he felt none of it now. He reached in and pulled out the one thing inside of it. A photograph.

Two women stood side by side. One of the women was Aunt Emma, standing beside a taller woman who was either quite fat or about to have a baby. Both women were smiling, certainly he couldn't see that either of them had a care in the world. He brought the photo closer to better see the other woman. Was she Patrick's mother?

Slipping the photo back in the handbag, Peter placed it carefully back into the wardrobe and closed the doors. He leaned against it to take stock. He'd found a photo of Aunt Emma and a pregnant woman, but that wasn't proof of wrongdoing.

Was he the one who was wrong? He'd die of embarrassment if anyone caught him going through Aunt Emma's things. Especially if she ultimately turned out to be Patrick's mother, and he had made a mess of things.

But he wasn't wrong. He knew it.

The only other place Peter thought he could check, because he wasn't going through anyone's undergarments to save his life, was under the bed. He dropped to his knees, flattened himself, and looked around. Nothing. He scooted out and flipped over onto his back and looked up at the mattress frame. Bingo. A bulky brown envelope was tucked between the frame and the bottom mattress. Eagerly, he slipped out from under the bed and lifted up the mattress.

He knew he didn't have much time left. The last of the afternoon sun was streaming in the window. With the black out, he'd have no chance of turning on the light and getting away with it. The envelope wasn't sealed, which eased Peter's conscience to no end. He untied the fastening and spilled the papers out onto the rug.

The top papers were business letters. His eyes scanned them quickly. To his mind there was nothing remarkable in the first few letters. He continued to sift through them but froze when he got midway through the pile. German. Half the letters were in German.

He couldn't read the language but he recognized the way the words looked. German words were uncommonly long, he knew that much. A sick feeling rolled around his stomach. Why did she have German letters in her room, hidden in her room, unless…. he clapped his hands over his mouth. Unless she was a spy? He truly felt sick now. Kidnapping would land Aunt Emma in a world of trouble but treason would land her in the gallows.

He reached into his pocket and pulled out a piece of paper and the stub of a pencil. As quickly as he was able, he scribbled down as many words as he could, knowing that it was woefully inadequate but it was all he had time for. A glance outside confirmed as much, he'd better put the papers away before Aunt Joanna came to draw the blackout curtains.

Once he'd tucked the envelope back into place, Peter stood at the door and looked around the room to make sure nothing was amiss. Everything looked in its proper place but nothing looked the same as it did when he'd first entered the room. Everything might look the same but it wasn't. Everything had changed. Aunt Emma was in more trouble then he'd ever be able to help her out of.

"PARDON ME, SIR, BUT I HAVE SOME QUESTIONS ABOUT YOUR SCHEDULE for the next few weeks. Might I have a word now?"

Malcolm, sitting at his desk, looked up at the young girl that stood in his office doorway. His eyes took in her far too skinny form, her pale complexion, and her hideous orange hair that was scraped back off her face. Good God, where did they get these ugly young women to fill the secretary pool? Was there an endless supply of them somewhere in London? He grimaced.

"I can come back later, Sir, if you prefer," she said.

Malcolm could hear the tremor in the girl's voice. He resisted the urge to say something scathing and watch her run for cover. He didn't have the time.

"Ask me now," he snapped. "But be quick about it."

"Yes, Sir." She consulted the schedule book that she was holding. "You've been invited to speak Tuesday next at a business luncheon for--"

"No, I don't have time next week. Decline the invitation and clear the rest of my schedule."

"But you have a very full schedule next week, Sir. Are you certain that you want every appointment canceled?"

Malcolm's palm itched with a desire to reach out and smack the timid expression straight off of her face. He knew well enough that his hand striking her face would sound like a cracking whip. Particularly satisfying would be the stunned, panicked expression in her eyes after she realized what had happened. He'd have to pass this time though, he was due for a luncheon meeting.

"Cancel everything." He stood and turned his back to the girl. He let his gaze wander over the courtyard below his office for a long moment before he turned back to her. "I'm going away next week. I fancy a few days by the sea."

CHAPTER 10

Three dances with tipsy airmen, two kisses neatly dodged, and one headache later, Emma slipped out of the noisy makeshift dance hall in search of a quiet spot to catch her breath.

She glanced briefly over her shoulder as she left, feeling slightly guilty at leaving Stuart without telling him she was going. He was buzzed from all of the lager he'd put back and probably wouldn't notice she was gone for hours yet. All the better, she wanted to be alone.

Two young women in the entryway laughed as they shook the rain from their umbrellas. They smiled at Emma as she passed them. Their young and eager expressions made her feel old. Not that long ago those two young carefree girls could have been her and Patricia. The memory of how innocent they'd been, and how they'd believed that life was nothing but an adventure, seemed unbearably sad now.

She headed in the direction of the office she shared with Andrej but stopped. Unless he was at the cottage, he would likely be in the office working. She could head back to the cottage but that held little appeal if the children weren't there. She glanced up the massive staircase in front of her. Hadn't she seen a small sitting room that had been turned into a lounge on the second floor? Perhaps it was empty.

At the top of the stairs she hesitated. The corridor was empty and only a few small lights shone. Was that music she heard? She strained to listen. Yes, it was. Classical music was coming from one of the rooms at the end of the corridor. The sadness and the longing in the music called to Emma. Following the haunting melody, she continued down the corridor until she reached a door that was slightly ajar.

She slipped in the room, unsure of what she'd find. Several seconds passed before her eyes adjusted to the darkness. Only a single candle on a far corner table was lit. At first she'd thought she'd find a phonograph playing but she saw someone sitting at the piano. Although the room was in shadows, she instantly knew it was Andrej by the breadth of his shoulders.

Reason told her to turn and go, but the beauty of the music compelled her to stay. The passion with which Andrej played pulled at her heart. She'd never heard anything so exquisite, so magnificent, in all of her life. A moment more was all she wanted and then she'd leave before he knew she was there.

Without warning, Andrej stopped playing and turned around to look in her direction. "Emma?" His voice sounded uncertain.

"Yes, Andrej, it's me." She remained standing by the door. "Forgive me, I didn't know you were here. I heard the music and wanted to hear more."

He was quiet for so long that Emma worried he might be annoyed by her intrusion. But when he spoke she heard no trace of anger in his words.

"Would you like me to play for you?"

"Please do," she answered. "I'd enjoy that."

He motioned toward the sofa next to the table with the candle. Emma slipped off her shoes and settled onto the sofa, drawing her legs up under her. Once she was still, Andrej began to play. Emma easily surrendered to the magic of the moment. In the beauty of the music she found refuge from her worries, in Andrej's presence she felt free of fear.

She didn't recognize the piece Andrej was playing but it was, without question, without parallel, the most beautiful composition she'd ever heard. She was sorry when it came to an end.

"Was that Mozart?" she asked.

"No." Andrej was so soft-spoken that Emma barely heard him. "I wrote this piece."

Emma was speechless. Nearly. "Oh, Andrej, it was brilliant. Magnificent even. I could feel the sadness and the loneliness but I could feel the hope in it as well." She held her hands over her heart. "I can't find the words to tell you how amazing it was."

Andrej turned to face her. "I'm glad you liked it." She couldn't make out his expression in the semi-darkness but the vulnerability in his voice tore at her heart.

"I loved it. I had no idea you wrote music."

"Tell me what you think my life was like in London."

Emma smiled. "I imagine that you have a tiny flat in Chelsea, top floor of course, with a temperamental lift. And you have students coming at all hours of the day and night. Your flat is tidy, perhaps you have a plant, maybe even a cat, and books and music everywhere. In the evenings, after your last student is gone, I imagine you go round to your favorite pub and sit with the same friends you've had for years and years. Am I close?"

"No." His voice sounded wistful. "That's not it at all."

"Not even a little?"

Silence answered her. It didn't escape her notice that when Andrej was working he was always in the moment, focused, his words clear and direct. But any mention of the past seemed to rob him of his certainty.

Emma patted the cushion beside her. "Come and tell me about your life, Andrej," she coaxed. "Please."

He did as she bid, slowly and tentatively. He settled onto the farthest edge of the sofa and avoided looking at her. Instead, he studied his hands.

Emma, in turn, studied him. The sight of him softened her heart. She'd come to depend on the warmth she felt when she was with him and the sense of safety she felt cloaked in when he was near. It was abundantly clear, however, that he shared none of her ease in being together.

"Would you like me to find Stuart for you?" Andrej asked.

The mention of Stuart felt like she'd been doused with cold water. She shook her head. "I don't want to go just yet."

"You're not afraid to be here with me?"

Emma was aghast at the suggestion. "No, of course not. I've never been afraid of you. Why would you say that?"

He refused to meet her eye. "The last time we were alone together I frightened you."

Emma shook her head vehemently. "No, no. You didn't. I might have been embarrassed that I was so forward with you but I wasn't afraid." She stopped, suddenly understanding that he'd misunderstood her shock at hearing Malcolm's message and assumed it had to do with his kiss. She wanted to explain, but how could she offer an explanation without mentioning Malcolm?

Instead, she reached out and took Andrej's hand in hers. She traced her fingers lightly over his palm. "Hands that create such beauty could never hurt me." She released his hand and sat back. "I'm sorry if I made you believe that."

Andrej shook his head, a rueful smile on his lips. "Let that be the last apology between us Emma."

She nodded. "Agreed."

"Shall we head back to the cottage?" he asked.

She shook her head. "Not just yet. It feels peaceful here. I want to stay a bit longer."

Andrej reached for his jacket and laid it gently over her shoulders. "I don't want you to be cold."

She smiled gratefully.

The candle flickered dramatically before it went out. Andrej moved to find another but Emma put out her arm to stop him. "I don't mind the dark."

"Tell me what you want, Emma, and it shall be yours."

She hesitated only for a moment. "I want you to sit here next to me for now. Patrick is with Iris tonight and I don't want to be alone."

In answer, Andrej moved closer to Emma and drew her against him. She settled her head on his chest. He gently stroked her hair, and Emma felt much of the tension and fear she'd carried for so long leave her body.

"Are you going to tell me about your life before you arrived here?" Emma asked.

"Must I?"

She nodded. "Is there something you're hiding?"

"Yes."

His tone cautioned Emma that he was wary of confiding in her. She gently placed her hand on his knee.

"I want to know more about you, Andrej. But only what you want to tell me."

She waited, listening as the clock ticked the moments away.

"You'd never heard my name before I introduced myself on the train?" His voice was low, cautious, guarded even.

"Should I have?"

He chuckled softly. "What sort of music do you listen to?"

"I enjoy Bing Crosby and the Andrews Sisters, anything new that I can dance to."

"Not classical music?"

"No, but then I've never before heard anything as magnificent as the music you played tonight."

"You liked it that much?" He sounded pleased, which made Emma smile.

"I loved it. It was enchanting." She snuggled into him. "I could listen to you play forever and still not have heard enough. Tell me how long you've been teaching."

"I'm not a music teacher. I am a concert pianist."

"Are you famous?" The way he played so masterfully, she wouldn't be surprised.

Andrej made a non-committal sound.

"Are you?" she prompted. "Tell me about your career."

When Andrej began to speak, Emma closed her eyes and listened as he told her of his passion for music, of his travels and the countries his tours had taken him too. She'd rarely left London so his tales of Buenos Aires, Tokyo, and Sydney enthralled her. She loved listening to his melodic accented English and, despite his deep voice, his words were gently spoken. Safe in his arms, she could feel herself being lulled into a state of deep relaxation.

"All of your travels sound magical," she spoke in almost a whisper. "Tell me, if you could be anywhere in the world tonight where would you most like to be?"

"Nowhere else but here, Emma." He lifted her hand and brushed a kiss across her wrist. "Nowhere else but with you."

SHE WASN'T AFRAID OF HIM. ANDREJ FELT AS IF A THOUSAND POUND weight had been lifted off of his heart. He glanced down at Emma, now asleep. For the first time, he felt as if he had everything he could ever want from life right in front of him.

He wasn't a fool though. He knew that when Emma awoke the spell would be broken and they could go back to belonging in two separate worlds. Which was how it should be. As clearly as if it had been yesterday, and not decades ago, Andrej heard the last words his mother had whispered before she'd left him, "You don't belong with our family, Andrej."

This time at Laurel Cottage, the time spent working with Emma and being around the children, had been a gift to him. He'd been made to feel like a normal person. He'd cherish the memory of each moment after he went back to his lonely life.

Emma. God, but how he'd miss her. Her devotion to the children amazed him. It also worried him. Not the way she cared for Peter and Lily. She was incredibly loving towards them. They were fortunate children indeed to be under her care. No, it was Patrick that worried Andrej. The way Emma loved and cared for him with such tender-ness...she was more devoted than any mother he could imagine.

He leaned down and gently kissed the top of her head. Gently, so as not to wake her, he tightened his hold on her, wishing that doing so was enough to keep her safe from the trouble she had gotten herself in by taking Patrick away from his mother. Andrej couldn't explain his certainty, but he now believed that Peter was right. Emma wasn't Patrick's mother. Which meant that someone somewhere was looking for their son. And the woman who'd taken him.

Emma stirred in his arms.

"Rest now, my dear," he whispered soothingly.

The thought of Emma facing kidnapping charges tore at his heart. She must know the trouble that awaited her. The wild fear he'd seen in her eyes that day at the cottage when she'd received the phone message told him. She knew.

Once again, his mind went back to the message that Lily had relayed to Emma. 'I think of my baby's mother often'. The word choice sounded awkward to his ear, but perhaps it was because English wasn't his native language. What meaning could there be in the way those words were arranged?

Why had Emma taken Patrick? He'd asked himself the question dozens of times but could never arrive at a satisfactory answer. He couldn't fool himself into believing that Patrick was an orphan and Emma had stepped forward to care for him. There'd be no need for secrecy if that were true.

Why had Emma begged him that first night in London to take the baby to an orphanage if something happened to her? She'd said she and Patrick were all alone in the world. Was there no one, not one friend or family member, that she'd trust to care for the baby? Why hadn't she mentioned her parents in Canada? Her lies. Her fears. Her reaction to the phone message. It made no sense.

What could he do? Confront her? She'd lie. She'd say whatever she thought necessary to protect Patrick. Directly approaching her would accomplish nothing. Another choice was to do nothing. But this was out of the question.

He cared too deeply for her to let her destroy her life by continuing to go along on the path of deceit she'd chosen. No. Far better that she hated him for his involvement in finding Patrick's true parents. He couldn't stand by and watch her destroy her future.

Since the direct approach was out of the question, Andrej knew that only left him one choice. He'd need to spend every moment he could with Emma, win her trust and then…he'd ask her to marry him.

The idea surprised him but it was perfect. By marrying Emma he could perhaps be able to protect her, and extend that protection to Patrick until he was returned to his real family. So far as he knew, Emma had little money to buy her way out of trouble. He, however, had ample funds to provide the best legal counsel available. Riches were no guarantee that he could keep Emma out of jail but having money might be helpful if things were handled carefully.

Emma was going to hate him. She would loathe him when she learned that he'd betrayed the very trust he was going to work to win. But it was the only way to save her from herself. And it would be worth enduring her hatred to know that he'd saved her from prison.

Peter would be a natural ally. Good hearted, naturally intuitive, and highly intelligent, the lad was just the person Andrej needed to help him. It hadn't escaped his notice that Peter watched Emma with a careful curiosity. What was it that Peter knew? Was the extent of it the one conversation he claimed to overhear or was there something more he knew? Andrej was uncomfortable with the thought of using the lad to gain information but he had little choice. Time was not on his side.

Andrej leaned further back into the sofa and tightened his hold on Emma. He fought against the tiredness that pulled at his eyelids. He didn't want to waste a moment of this chance to hold her in his arms. He wished he could hold her forever, but there would be no forever for them. Not once she found out that he was the reason she was going to lose Patrick. She wouldn't even want to look at him after she discovered the betrayal he was planning. He'd then have to settle for holding the memory of her in his heart.

"Emma, wake up. Emma, can you hear me?" Will shook her shoulder with an increasing intensity. There wasn't time to be patient or gentle. Not until they found the boy.

Emma's eyelids fluttered open and she looked around the room, disoriented he didn't doubt.

"Where am I? What time is it?" She sat up and looked at Will in surprise. "Where's Andrej?"

"He's ringing the Police Station."

Will watched as a dawning horror spread across Emma's expression. The poor girl. He knelt beside her. "We're going to find him, my dear. I promise."

Emma shot to her feet. An anguished heart-wrenching sob escaped her, a horrendous sound that Will hadn't heard since he'd had to tell Joanna their son had been killed in France. He placed a comforting arm around her trembling shoulders.

"What time...how long...when did you notice he was gone?"

"Joanna discovered him missing a couple of hours ago and I've been looking for you since." Will tightened his hold on her as her face grew ashen. "When we didn't see you last night, we thought perhaps the little chap was with you somewhere."

They both turned as Andrej replaced the receiver and joined them.

"Constable Allen is going to meet us at the cottage shortly." He took his coat and placed it over Emma's trembling shoulders.

Will stood back as Andrej pulled Emma into his arms. "I'm going back to the cottage now to ring some home guard members and organize a search," Will told them. The frenzied look in Emma's eyes told him that there was nothing he could say to help her. He'd best leave that to Andrej.

CHAPTER 11

*E*mma leaned into Andrej. "Help me find him," she begged. She clutched his shirt, panic threatening to choke her. "Please help me."

Andrej held her at arm's length, his hands on her shoulders. "Think, Emma, where might he be? Do you have any idea?" His voice was rough, insistent, and held none of the warmth that it had only hours before. When she didn't answer immediately, he gave her shoulders a gentle shake. "There must be something you know that can help us find him."

Malcolm. Emma's fear transformed into a towering rage. Malcolm, the bloody bastard, had her baby. She'd kill him. She'd find him and kill him. She should have known that he would stop at nothing to get Patrick away from her. He didn't want the baby. If Patrick were to die, then Malcolm's life would be all the easier. She would put nothing past him. If he could kill a mother, why not a child?

The thought of her precious baby in the hands of such a monster… she buried her face in her hands.

"Emma," Andrej said, his voice stern, "Pull yourself together. You have to help us." He lowered her arms, took her face in his hands and forced her to meet his eye. "We'll find him, but I need you to stay strong. Do you think you're able to walk down to the cottage? We need to talk to the police."

Something in his eyes broke through Emma's panic. She needed to pull herself together, immediately. "I'm ready," she heard herself say, although her voice sounded far away, as if someone else was speaking the words. She slipped her arm through his and allowed him to lead her out of the room. She doubted she'd have the strength to walk on her own.

When they arrived at the cottage, a constable was in the kitchen talking to Will. Joanna rushed to Emma's side when she caught sight of her. She drew her into a brief but ferocious hug before leading her to a chair. She then stood beside her, a reassuring hand on Emma's shoulder.

The constable, an elderly man with silver hair and dark bushy eyebrows, drew out a pad of paper and looked at Emma. "Mrs. Bradley, you're the lad's guardian, I'm told?"

Emma's head snapped up. "I'm his mother."

Silence filled the kitchen. Emma watched in a daze as Will and Joanna exchanged startled glances. Andrej wore the same puzzled expression the others did.

"I received a call that a young lad has gone missing," Constable Allen said. "I was under the impression the boy was an evacuee."

Emma gasped. Peter? Oh, God, it was Peter who was missing? She'd assumed it was Patrick.

"Emma." The commanding tone of Andrej's voice made her meet his eye. "Patrick's safe."

She nodded her understanding. "I thought it was Patrick." She wiped away her tears with the back of her hand. But her relief turned to horror at the thought of Peter out somewhere by himself. She turned to Joanna. "Where is Patrick?"

"He's safe with Iris, dear."

"You're sure, you're absolutely certain?"

Joanna nodded. "She said she will keep him until we find Peter. She said to tell you that she won't let him out of her sight for a single moment. She's asked her brother to come stay with them. Mind you, he's a big man, and a policeman himself."

Emma nodded, grateful beyond words that Patrick was safe. Iris' message told her that her friend understood the threat Malcolm posed. She pressed her fingers to her temples, as if to align her thoughts. It was Peter she needed to think of now. "Where is Lily?"

"Who is Lily?" Constable Allen asked. He looked at each of them in turn. "Someone has to give me some information right now. Each moment the boy is gone is going to make it harder for us to find him."

They all began to talk at once. He held up his hand, "One at a time. Who can describe him?"

As Will answered the policeman's questions, Emma turned to Joanna. "Is Lily with Peter?"

Joanna shook her head. "No, she's up in her room sobbing her little heart out. Apparently, they had a nasty row and Peter stormed out. She thought he'd just come down here to pout but he must have left. Will and I were still asleep and we didn't hear the door close."

A horrifying thought suddenly occurred to Emma. She felt her stomach turn over. "Were there any signs that Peter was taken against his will?" Was Malcolm somehow involved with Peter's disappearance?

Will was the first to answer her question. "No, it appears as if he left willingly. We just don't know why. Or where he went."

Emma avoided meeting Andrej's eye. She had an uncomfortable feeling that he could follow her thoughts. It was too soon to say anything to anyone about Malcolm, at least for Patrick's sake. Unless it would help them find Peter, she didn't want Malcolm brought into this. If he, in fact, had taken Peter, she'd know soon enough. "I need to see Lily. May I go upstairs and speak with her?" she asked the constable.

"In a moment." He glanced at the notebook in his hand and re-read his notes. "I would like to hear what the girl has to say myself. After we're done speaking with her we need to organize and have you split up." He looked at Joanna. "Please fetch the girl."

When Lily entered the room, she ran straight into Emma's arms. Tears poured down her cheeks and she clung to Emma.

"Lily, my love, everything's going to turn out alright." She drew the girl onto her lap. "Do you have any idea at all where Peter might have gone?"

Lily shook her head emphatically. "None whatsoever."

"Do you know why he might have gone off without a word?"

Lily's lower lip trembled. "It's all my fault, Aunt Emma." She looked at the other adults in the room before turning back to Emma. She lowered her voice. "We had a terrible argument. I told him to go away but I meant from the room...not from the house."

Emma gently rocked her. "It's not your fault, love. Peter has a mind of his own, we all know that. And he knows you love him, even if you did have words."

Constable Allen came over to them and drew up a chair opposite Emma.

"Lily, we want to find your brother but we need your help." He spoke to her in a calm, soothing manner that Emma appreciated. "What was Peter wearing the last time you saw him? Was he wearing his night clothes?"

Lily shook her head. "He was wearing his regular clothes. But when he left the room he took his pillow, which made me think that he was going to sleep in the sitting room." She stopped and frowned.

"What is it, Lily?" Emma asked. "Did you think of something else that could help us?"

"The only other thing he had besides his pillow was his small notebook. You know the one he always wrote--" She stopped talking abruptly, which caused the adults to exchange curious glances.

"What did he write in it, Lily?" Emma prompted.

"Lots of things, whatever he was thinking about, I suppose. Last night he was talking about some notes he'd written in German."

"Was he talking about the phrases I taught him?" Andrej asked.

Constable Allen turned to Andrej, shock clear upon his face. "You're teaching the children German?" Disapproval was evident in the way he spat out the last word.

Emma ignored this. This wasn't the time to discuss the language lessons. "Did you hear Peter come back in the room again after that?"

"No. After he left, I fell asleep fairly quickly."

Andrej came over and knelt before them so that he was at Lily's eye level. "Do you think Peter would try to go to London?"

Lily cocked her head to the side and thought for a moment. "No, not without me, he wouldn't. He didn't have any money for the train. Besides, Peter wouldn't do anything to make Mummy angry. She'd kill him if he--" her eyes darted over to the policeman, a worried look on her face. "She wouldn't really kill him, of course. That's not what I meant."

Constable Allen smiled at Lily. "I have children and grandchildren of my own so I know exactly what you meant, my dear."

After a quick conference with Andrej and Will, he turned to Joanna and Emma. "We've got a man at the Manor to search there. I'll send another man around to the train station and one to the hospital."

Upon hearing the word 'hospital', Lily burst into fresh tears. Emma fought the urge to do the same. The thought of Peter, sweet, mischievous, precious Peter, injured made Emma's heart ache so badly she could barely breathe.

"Where can I go to look for him?" she asked.

"You need to stay here," Andrej answered before the constable could speak.

"I agree with the foreign gentleman," Constable Allen said. "Mr. Metcalf will meet with off-duty home guard members and organize a search of the beach and pier areas. Mrs. Metcalf, you'd best head into town and start asking shopkeepers to spread the word so people can be on the lookout for him. Your husband can drop you off there on his way." He looked at Emma. "Mrs. Bradley, I'd recommend you stay here with the young miss just in case Peter should return home."

"I will head out to the air field," Andrej offered. "Peter has mentioned several times that he'd like to see the planes there."

"Fine idea," the policeman agreed. "I'll phone ahead and ask that they admit you."

Moments later, Emma waited by the front door for Andrej. She'd seen Will and Joanna off with Constable Allen, and she'd sent Lily upstairs to wash her face.

She jumped when Andrej came up behind her and placed his hands on her shoulders. He drew her to him and laid his cheek on her head. "I didn't mean to startle you." His words were but a whisper. "We'll have Peter home tonight, I promise."

A tear slid down Emma's face, quickly followed by yet another. "Why wasn't I here last night, Andrej?" She turned to look up at him. "If I had, then Peter would be safe."

"You can't know that." He cupped her face with one hand and gently wiped away her tears with the other. He leaned down and placed a gentle kiss on her forehead. "He's a smart, resourceful boy and he'd have found a way to sneak out if he wanted, you know that. But also remember that means he's smart enough to stay safe. Yes?"

Emma nodded her head, unable to speak through her sadness, her fear, and now her gratitude. She looked into Andrej's eyes and mouthed the words 'thank you'.

A loud knock on the other side of the door startled them both. Emma threw it open. "Peter, thank heavens you've--" Her face fell when she saw Stuart standing there, rubbing his temples.

"Stuart," she stood back so he could enter. "What are you doing here?"

Stuart brushed past them both and leaned against the wall. "Emma, I've just heard that the little chap has run off. I thought I'd wait here with you. I've got an awful headache from last night, must have drank too much." He closed his eyes and groaned. "I wouldn't turn down a cup of tea."

Unsympathetic, Emma waved him in the direction of the kitchen. "Put the kettle on yourself, then. But after a cuppa, you'd best be prepared to join the search party."

She turned back to wish Andrej luck in his search but he was already gone. She closed her eyes and issued a swift but fervent prayer that he would find Peter before something unthinkable happened.

PETER'S STOMACH GROWLED. HIS BEST GUESS TOLD HIM IT WAS PAST noon. He'd left the cottage without taking food, afraid any noise he might make in the kitchen would awaken someone. Truth told, he'd expected to be back at Laurel Cottage well before tea time. What he hadn't counted on was the trouble he'd have slipping into the building where the German POWs were held.

He sat down on the grass beneath a tall tree. It was doubtful anyone would see him in the shady spot he'd chosen. His stomach growled again. Never again would he venture out without at least an apple in his pocket.

He looked through the barbed wire at the building about fifty meters in front of him. Perhaps it had been a school before. It was three stories high with windows that were almost completely boarded up. Only the very tops of the windows were left open, just enough for light and air but no man, or boy for that matter, would be able to squeeze either in or out. The front door was guarded by two men with large guns. He imagined the other doors were just as heavily guarded. As well they ought to be, Peter reasoned, there were enough Nazis in the sky. Nobody wanted to see them running loose on the ground.

Except for himself, of course. He just wanted to see one, briefly for a moment, and definitely from the opposite side of the barbed wire. The only good thing he could think to say about Germans was that they spoke German. He desperately wanted someone to look at the notes he'd copied from the letters. He needed someone to read the words and tell him they meant nothing of consequence.

Last night he'd considered asking Mr. Van der Hoosen to take a look at the letter but he'd been unable to find him. Then Lily told him that Aunt Emma hadn't come home, despite the dance having been over for a long while. His sister had thought perhaps, since they were both gone, that they were on a date. That was when the horrible idea occurred to him that perhaps Aunt Emma and Mr. Van der Hoosen were in cahoots.

If the two were involved in a spy ring it would at least explain that certain something between them. He didn't know what to call it, some sort of special connection. It hadn't made any sense before. But when Aunt Emma and Mr. Van der Hoosen were in a room together the air had a certain crinkly feeling to it. Was crinkly even a word? Probably not. He was sure that Lily would have a girly word for it but that was the least of his problems right now. If they were spies, there was no end to the subterfuge and chaos they could create by miscalculating or mistranslating the maps they were always working on.

Peter knew he should be angry, better yet, he should hate them both. But it was hard. Aunt Emma was so kind to them, she was a great deal of fun. Mr. Van der Hoosen, although he acted like he was never sure where he fit in, had proven to be a good sort.

Last night he'd started to tell Lily about his idea but she hadn't even let him get to the part about the letters before she'd turned bossy on him. She'd called him a wretched boy just out to make trouble. That still stung. He wasn't going to easily forgive her.

His head snapped up when he heard voices. He jumped up and scooted around the back of the tree. Peering out around it, he could see one of the guards patrolling the enclosed yard. An enormous Alsatian was by the guard's side. Peter's stomach turned over. The dog was looking straight at him. It didn't bark, although it stopped walking. His handler tugged on the dog's lead, urging it ahead.

With the dog reluctantly on its way back to the guard house, Peter peeked back around the edge of the tree. Before he could make up his mind what to do next, the guard blew a whistle. A side door opened and out poured close to fifty men, all marching in a single file.

Peter eyed what he presumed were German prisoners. He silently thanked fate. Now all he had to do was hope they marched close to the fence. He watched as the men walked around the field twice. On their second pass they marched closer to the fence. Peter was surprised how young some of them seemed. One man looked over as he marched by and did a double take when he spied Peter. Peter put his finger to his lips. The prisoner nodded.

Another whistle sounded and the men began to jog. When he came close to the fence this time, the man didn't turn his head or make eye contact but he casually lifted his finger, making the universal sign for 'wait a moment'. Peter didn't have to wait long. Yet another whistle blew and suddenly a handful of footballs appeared. The prisoners began kicking them back and forth.

After several very long moments, Peter's prisoner ran by the fence, pretended to fall, and pointed at his shoe when the guard motioned for him to rejoin the others. He dallied over tying his shoe.

"Who are you?" the man called in English. "What do you want?"

Awfully cheeky question for someone behind a wire fence, Peter couldn't help but think. At least the man spoke English. That was going to make things easier.

"I need help reading something in German."

The prisoner took off his shoe and pretended to dump out a rock. "Do you have any food?"

The question surprised Peter. He glanced up at the men running back and forth chasing after the football. None of them were plump. Some looked terribly skinny. They were a scraggly lot.

"No, I don't. I'm sorry." He was too. "Can you help me with these words?" He'd come too far, and was in too much trouble, to get off track now. Luckily for them both, the guard was watching the man but didn't seem inclined to move from where he stood.

"You must agree to do something for me first." The German peeled off his socks and shook them out, buying time.

"I can't get you out of there if that's what you're wanting," Peter said.

The prisoner smiled wistfully, "I wouldn't dare to hope. No, what I want is to give you an address in Dublin. You must write a letter and tell them you saw me and that I'm well."

"Is that some sort of code?" Peter asked. "I won't be part of any Nazi plot."

"Nein. This person can get word to my mother in Hamburg that I am safe." He looked over at the guard house and back to Peter. "You will do this?"

Peter nodded. What choice did he have? He absolutely had to know if Aunt Emma's letters meant she was a spy. He scribbled down the name and address the man told him. Then, unable to read the German words to the man, he rapidly spelled out word after word.

"Who is this letter from?" the prisoner asked.

"That doesn't concern you," Peter said. "I want to know the meaning of it all."

"If the person who wrote it is English then they mean to betray your government. They speak of offering assistance to the new Nazi government."

Peter frowned. "What new Nazi government?"

"After Germany successfully invades England there will be no more King, no more Parliament. England will belong to Germany."

"Never," Peter cried indignantly. He jumped to his feet and stepped out from behind the tree to face the older man. Too late, he realized that he'd caught the attention of the guard.

The prisoner looked over his shoulder. He quickly tied both shoes and stood. He started to jog back toward his fellow inmates. "Remember your promise, boy."

Peter took one look at the Alsatian now running towards the fence and he took off as fast as he was able. He ran blindly through the wooded area, away from the road by which he'd come. He ran as if doing so would put distance between his problems and himself. He couldn't run far enough or fast enough.

It was only when he stopped to catch his breath, bent over double and panting for air, that Peter realized he had no idea where he was. He spun around but saw nothing other than trees, woods, and a gray sky that threatened rain, a threat that was soon enough delivered upon. The first raindrop fell just as Peter's first tear did.

CHAPTER 12

*E*mma leaned her forehead against the window pane, grateful for the cool sensation against her flushed skin. For the hundredth time, her eyes scanned the front lawn. She desperately wished Peter would come straggling up the drive, feet dragging and head downcast, fully aware of the trouble he was in. In the hours she'd been awaiting news from the searchers, her emotions had swung wildly between fear and anger. They always ended back at fear. *Please God, just let him be safe.*

"Emma, come away from the window," Stuart called from where he sat on the sofa. "Standing there isn't going to make Peter come home any sooner."

"Then what will?" Emma whirled around, endlessly frustrated by Stuart's calm demeanor. "Why don't you go and help search for him?"

"Where?" Stuart looked up, genuinely puzzled. "He's probably off chasing rabbits, or sparrows, or he's gone to meet up with a chum somewhere. Why do you have to assume he's in trouble?"

Because an evil man hates me, she longed to blurt out. Because I know a man who has poison running through his veins. Because I alone have proof he's a treasonous bastard and he'll stop at nothing to hurt the people I care about. Nothing. "Because there is a war on,

Stuart," she said. "Because Peter's a little boy and he shouldn't be so far from home. What if there's an air raid? What if he isn't back before it's dark?"

Stuart came to stand beside her, awkwardly placing a hand on her shoulder. But she shrugged him off. She didn't want his comfort. She wanted Peter home.

At the sound of crunching gravel, Emma flew to the window. A taxi was at the front door. Not waiting to see who would alight, she ran to the door and threw it open.

It was Andrej. Without Peter. Emma's heart sank. She watched as he spoke to the driver, who in turn cut the motor and pulled out a newspaper.

His expression thunderous, Andrej strode toward Emma, caught her under the elbow, and propelled her into the sitting room. Speechless, she didn't resist. His anger was so palpable it reminded her of the night in London when he'd slammed the soldier up against a wall. She wasn't frightened of him, but she did fear the news that had angered him so.

His eyes landed on Stuart. "Go," he ordered.

Stuart leapt to his feet. "I say, old chap, what is wrong?"

"What is wrong?" Andrej spluttered. "Peter is missing. God only knows where he is or what will happen to him if we don't find him before dark. We've only got five or so hours until the light is gone." He took a menacing step toward Stuart. "Get out there and help find that boy."

Stuart's casual demeanor evaporated before Emma's eyes. "Where do you want me to start looking, Sir?"

"Clear your absence with Wing Commander Blythe first. See if he has suggestions, if not, find someone familiar with this area and ask if there are any abandoned buildings that a boy Peter's age could get to on foot. Now go."

Stuart did as he was bid with barely a backwards glance at Emma. As soon as the door slammed shut behind him, she stepped away from Andrej. "What have you found out? Has anyone at least seen Peter?"

"I'm not here to answer questions, Emma. I'm here to ask them."

"What are you talking about?" She took several steps backwards, away from the questions she feared were coming.

"Enough," he held up his hand. "You tell me whatever it is you know, or whatever it is you fear, right now. We don't have time for you to keep information to yourself."

"I don't know anything about where Peter is, Andrej. I swear I don't."

"What game is this you are playing? What has to happen before you tell me what you're hiding?"

"I am not--" She cut off the lie that automatically sprang to her lips. She *was* hiding something. But she was only doing what she had to do to protect Patrick. Andrej had no right to accuse her of hindering the search for Peter. She stood defiantly before him. "I am not withholding anything about Peter's disappearance."

"Tell me what you *are* withholding. Let me be the judge."

Judge? How dare he? She brushed past him, determined to leave the room, but he caught her arm and whirled her back around to face him.

"Where do you think you are going?"

"To find Peter." She could barely make herself say the words. She met his icy gaze, her own eyes blazing. "I'm not wasting another moment listening to your accusations. You don't have any idea what you're talking about."

"Oh, Emma, I know more than you think."

She wrenched her arm from his grasp. She fought an intense desire to cry, her tears wouldn't help Peter. "Don't you try to insinuate anything like that ever again. I won't tolerate it."

"You won't tolerate it?" Andrej choked out the words. "This isn't about you, Emma. It isn't about Patrick, or his father. It's about Peter. You owe it to him to tell me who you think may have taken him."

"I don't think anyone has taken Peter." She issued a silent prayer that her words would turn out to be true. "For some reason I can't fathom, he's gone off on his own. It doesn't even matter right now why he left. The only thing that matters is that we find him before nightfall." She grabbed her coat off of the rack and slipped her arms into the sleeves.

"You're not leaving the cottage, Emma. Not until you give me something, some idea who is involved. Until then you're staying here."

"The hell I will." Under normal circumstances she'd be horrified to hear herself use such language but she was beyond caring.

"I'll never forgive you if you could have prevented this, Emma, so help me God."

Waves of anger, fear, and guilt washed over Emma. She grabbed a hold of the door handle, as much for support as to open it. She leaned against it for a moment before she turned back to look at him. It took her a moment to find her voice. "Lily is upstairs. You stay here with her. I'm going to find Peter."

"I'm not upstairs."

They both whirled around to find Lily standing on the bottom step of the staircase. Her tear-stained face was drawn.

"Did I hear Mr. Van der Hoosen's voice?"

"Yes, Lily, I'm here." Andrej moved to Emma's side.

"Have you found any sign of Peter?"

Lily's hopeful expression tore at Emma's heart.

"No, we are still searching," Andrej told her. When he spoke to the girl, his voice was soft and gentle, a world away from the rough tone he used with Emma moments ago.

Lily walked past them both and looked out the same window Emma had been in front of the entire morning. "It's raining," she said softly. "Peter doesn't have his coat or his gas mask." She wiped away fresh tears. "Will we find him?"

Andrej spoke before Emma was able to find words to reassure her.

"I promise you, Lily, I won't return to the cottage without your brother." Andrej reached down and smoothed her hair, as gentle a gesture as Emma had ever seen. "I'm leaving now to go and bring Peter home."

In answer, Lily threw her arms around Andrej's waist. "Thank you."

Andrej extricated himself from her embrace with a few last reassuring words before he strode from the room. Emma winced as the front door slammed shut behind him. The taxi's motor rumbled to life and its tires crunched the gravel as it headed away from the cottage.

Andrej's last words to her echoed in her head, 'I'll never forgive you, Emma, if you could have prevented this'. She put her hands over her aching heart. She'd never forgive herself either.

⁓

"TELL ME WHERE THE BOY IS."

"Nein."

"You're a fortunate man the guard is watching us," Andrej told the prisoner, speaking German in a low voice, his rage barely controlled. "Otherwise, I'd wring your neck without a single thought. You're wasting my time."

"Speak English, Sir," the guard called to him. He stood with his back to the wall, for all appearances supremely uninterested in their conversation. "It's tempting to mistreat the Jerrys but we don't need the Red Cross in here complaining."

"I am sure that wringing my neck would be in violation of the Geneva Convention." The prisoner studied his fingernails, his English impeccable, his manner cool.

"Your refusal to help is in violation of human nature," Andrej shot back. He'd been relieved when he'd received word that Peter had been spotted near the detention center. He was, however, at his wits end with the POW that had been seen speaking with Peter. The man absolutely refused to cooperate, that much was clear. Why he wouldn't help, Andrej couldn't fathom. An even bigger mystery was why Peter would have sought out a German prisoner in the first place.

"What did he say to you?" Andrej tried again.

The prisoner shrugged but remained silent.

"What did you say to him?"

Silence. Andrej slammed his fist down on the metal desk. "That child is out there alone and it's going to be dark soon. I need to find him. Did he say anything, anything at all, about where he was going?"

Andrej knew the prisoner was withholding something. He could sense the other man consider his words, which information to give and which to keep, but Andrej wanted to hear it all.

"This boy is your son, ja?"

"He is in my care," Andrej allowed.

"I have nothing to tell you about where he might be." He leaned forward and met Andrej's gaze without blinking. "But I will say this, when you find him you need to keep a better eye on him. A boy walking around asking questions about the things he was could get very badly hurt." He stood and motioned to the guard. "Take me back now."

Lost in an agony of frustration, Andrej watched as the German left the room without a backward glance. What on earth could Peter possibly be up to? What was he saying or doing that could endanger him? He walked out of the detention center feeling none of the hope that he'd entered it with. If anything, he was more frightened than he'd ever been.

EMMA REACHED FOR THE TELEPHONE RECEIVER BUT PULLED HER HAND back as if from hot coals rather a cold phone. The thought of talking to Malcolm made her ill. But she had to know if he was involved in Peter's disappearance. It wasn't as if he didn't know where she and Patrick were, she reminded herself. His phone message last month had been left to taunt her.

Before she could change her mind again, she grabbed the phone and asked the operator to put a call through to Malcolm's London office. An unfamiliar woman's voice answered the phone. The latest secretary, Emma soon realized, was not terribly bright. She was quick to give out details regarding Malcolm's schedule far more freely than Emma would have done.

"My employer's asked that I set up an appointment, perhaps next Thursday," Emma lied smoothly.

"Oh, dear, did I not mention that next week is impossible?" the woman at the other end of the phone said. "Mr. Shand-Collins has been at the seaside all week and he's to stay through next week as well."

Emma's stomach turned to stone. "The seaside? Does he have a conference in Blackpool?"

"No, I believe he said he fancied some time in Brighton."

Emma hung up the phone with a shaking hand. She covered her mouth with both hands, anxious to stifle the sound of her cries so that Lily wouldn't hear. Andrej had been right. This was her fault and Peter, poor, sweet little Peter, was caught in the middle. She felt hopeless. Almost.

Andrej, who was still out looking for Peter, was her last glimmer of hope. He was going to have to learn the truth now that she knew Malcolm was likely involved. She'd been a fool to believe that he would leave them alone.

If only she knew where Andrej was. She went back to the window. When he returned, she would tell him everything, starting with the fact that Patrick wasn't her son. Trusting anyone with her secret was terrifying but she owed it to Peter. She only hoped that in trying to help Peter, her decision wasn't going to hurt Patrick.

RAIN POURED DOWN AROUND ANDREJ AS HE SLOGGED THROUGH THE wooded area behind the POW detention center. After leaving his fruitless interview with the prisoner, he considered his next move. His first call was to Laurel Cottage to check in. A tearful Emma confirmed his fear, there'd been no word either of Peter. She'd attempted to pepper him with questions about where he'd looked, what he'd heard, and when he'd be back, but he'd cut her short. He couldn't shake the niggling feeling that she knew something that could help them. But this wasn't the time for thoughts of Emma now. He'd deal with her lies later.

The rain clouds obscured what was left of the late afternoon light. Visibility was rapidly worsening. Andrej tried to imagine what was going through Peter's mind. Where would the boy have decided to go? Where he'd gone was a mystery, so instead Andrej tried to understand the why. Why had Peter left without a word?

Because no one would listen to him. There was the plain, ugly truth. The boy had tried to talk to him numerous times, both directly and indirectly, about Emma and his concerns about Patrick's mother. Andrej hadn't listened or given any credence to his fears. Which made him just as guilty as Emma was for Peter's disappearance. He couldn't remember a time when he felt so disgusted with himself. He was a selfish bastard, more worried about his precious boundaries than the welfare of a child.

He continued onward through the downpour. Unsure precisely why, his instincts told him that Peter would not have headed for the road. Surely, if he had, there was a far greater chance he would have been spotted already. Andrej continued in the opposite direction. Not a house, not a barn, not even a field could be clearly seen through the thickening mist. Still, he kept on.

Nearly an hour later, Andrej realized he'd come upon a lake. Wiping the rain from his brow, he scanned the area and spotted a small building. Not big enough to be a proper building, he realized it was only a boathouse. Still, it warranted a quick search.

A closer inspection showed the boat house had long since been abandoned. Andrej pushed against the door. To his relief it swung open. Before his eyes could adjust to the dim interior, something barreled into him.

"Mr. Van der Hoosen," Peter cried. "I'm ever so happy to see you."

Andrej knelt down and held Peter at arm's length. "Thank heavens you're safe, Peter. Are you hurt?" As best he could tell in the dim light, aside from a shaky voice, Peter appeared unharmed.

"No, I'm not hurt." Peter stood back and wiped a tear away with the back of his hand. "But I am in a great deal of trouble, aren't I?"

Andrej nodded gravely.

"I knew it." Peter walked over to a bench and sat. He leaned back against the wall and closed his eyes.

Seeing Peter this silent unsettled Andrej. It was so unlike the boy.

He joined him on the bench, glad to be off of his feet, weak as he was with relief. He issued a silent prayer of gratitude that Peter was alive and well. But finding the words to thank the heavens and the words to say to Peter were two different things. The former came much easier than the latter.

The rain continued to pour down on the boathouse, showing little sign of letting up. Andrej waited for Peter to speak but, when the boy showed no inclination to initiate a conversation, Andrej couldn't wait any longer. "Peter, tell me why you left the cottage."

"Shouldn't I wait until everyone is gathered for the big meeting first?"

"What big meeting?"

"The one where Aunt Emma, Aunt Joanna, Uncle Will, and especially Lily, tell me how badly I've behaved by running off."

"You don't think they deserve an explanation after they've spent the day worrying about you?"

"Sometimes it's horrible having so many people worry about you."

Andrej couldn't speak for the lump in his throat. It was a thousand times worse not having anyone who cared about you. He knew all too well. "Would you rather not have anyone worry where you were and if you were safe?"

Peter was silent. Answer enough for Andrej. For the moment at least, he didn't want to push the lad too hard lest he clam up and not share why he had gone off in the first place. Gaining that information mattered more to Andrej than any apology.

"I'm sorry, Sir." Peter's voice was low and contrite.

"Apology accepted, Peter. I am far too relieved that you're safe to be cross with you." He reached over and ruffled the boy's hair. "Although I do want to know why you left without a word to anyone."

Peter's reticence puzzled Andrej. The compassionate part of him wanted to leave the subject alone and simply take Peter home. However, the German prisoner's warning about Peter being in danger played in his mind. Until today, he'd wanted to protect himself by staying as distant as possible from the other inhabitants of Laurel Cottage. But Peter's disappearance had changed everything.

Andrej no longer wanted to stand on the sidelines apart from the others. He couldn't. He cared too much for them all. Peter's safety, Lily's happiness, Patrick's future, and Emma…there were no words to describe how dear Emma was to him. At least not any words he could yet say aloud.

The first step to protecting them all was to learn what Emma was hiding. Starting with what Peter knew about it all. But not here or now.

Andrej stood. "Come, it's time we head home."

Peter glanced up, clearly surprised. "You're not going to ask me a million more questions?"

"Not a million, no. Not tonight anyway. But we need to get back so the others can know you're safe."

"It's raining still. And it's nearly dark. How will we see to find our way home?" Peter asked, his words laced with uncertainty.

"Let me worry about that, son." Andrej held out his hand and watched as the boy readily took it. "You just stay next to me and I'll sort it all out."

"Yes, Sir. But can I say one more thing?"

"Yes." Andrej waited patiently while Peter appeared to be carefully selecting his words.

"Aunt Emma had nothing to do with the reason I left the cottage." He looked up at Andrej, an eager expression on his face. "It was all me being naughty and there's nothing else to it."

"As you say, Peter." Andrej pulled open the door. "As you say."

The boy's words were all the confirmation he needed.

CHAPTER 13

"Can you imagine a more annoying younger brother, Peter?" Lily asked as she straightened the blankets and tucked them under his mattress. "Because I can't."

"I'm sorry, Lily. I know I was wrong."

She ignored his apology and continued on with her fussing. "I mean, seriously, Peter. Traipsing about in the woods in the dark and rain during the day while we were all worried sick…what were you thinking?" She sat at the foot of his bed and frowned at him.

Peter just wanted to sleep. The trip home had been long. Mr. Van der Hoosen had even carried him a great part of the way, something Peter would never admit to Lily. He was exhausted from the cold, the dark, and the rain.

"I want to sleep, Lily. Can we talk in the morning?"

"Of course, Peter. You're going to be doing plenty of talking in the morning. When Aunt Joanna and Uncle Will come home tomorrow you can apologize and explain everything to them."

Peter nodded his agreement. Fair enough.

"And Aunt Emma was so happy to see you that she let you off the hook. For tonight anyway. Tomorrow will be a different story."

"I know," Peter concurred. It was obvious he had to have one last conversation with Lily before she'd let him sleep. Not that he thought he could actually sleep. But he did need the quiet time to think of what to say, and not say, to the adults tomorrow so they wouldn't suspect what he'd really been up to.

It was all a jumbled mess in his head. Why was Aunt Emma pretending she was Patrick's mother? Were those letters hers? Was she a German spy? Or did they belong to someone else? Mr. Van der Hoosen, perhaps?

The idea made him feel ill. He liked Aunt Emma a great deal. In fact, he wished she really was his aunt. And he liked Mr. Van der Hoosen as well. He closed his eyes and groaned.

"What is it, Peter?" Lily asked. "Are you ill?"

"No, not exactly. I just want to sleep."

Lily nodded her understanding and went over to her bed. She pulled back the covers and slipped in. "I'm glad you're home safely." She yawned. After a moment she added, "I'm sure it will be quite a story you'll tell us tomorrow."

"That it will be." As soon as he thought of it anyway. His promise to the German prisoner popped into his mind. He rolled over. "Lily, do you have a stamp?"

"Yes, of course. I'll give it to you in the morning." She was quiet a moment. "Are you writing to reassure Mum that you're safe?"

"Something like that." Peter wondered about the prisoner's mother in Germany. Was she worried about her son? He supposed even Nazis worried. They'd certainly caused enough trouble for everyone. It seemed only fair they should worry as well.

One more thing was bothering him. Emma had fussed over him, cried a little, and hugged him countless times. Yet she hadn't said more than a few words to Andrej. Or he to her for that matter. But the way they kept looking at each other told him that something was going to happen tonight. He just hoped it wouldn't be a horrible row.

"WHAT ON EARTH DID HE HAVE TO SAY FOR HIMSELF?" IRIS DEMANDED, her tone equal parts relief and annoyance.

Emma shared her friend's consternation. "To tell you the truth, Lily and I were so relieved to see him home and unharmed that we didn't press for details. We fed him, gave him a warm bath, and he's tucked in bed now fast asleep."

"Who is 'we'?"

"Lily and I."

"Where are Will and Joanna?" Iris asked.

"In town. They're going to spend the night with friends. By the time I got word to them that Peter was safe, it was too dark for them to safely travel home."

"So, you're there alone with Andrej for the night?"

"The children are here."

"They're asleep you said?" Iris asked, feigning innocence, but Emma knew she was already fully aware they were asleep and would be for the night.

Emma sat down on the stairs and switched the phone to her other shoulder. A change of conversation was definitely in order. "I miss Patrick so terribly. I've never spent this much time away from him."

"He's fast asleep and so is Robert. So don't you dare show up here and disturb either one of them. I'll come round in the morning and bring him to you."

"Is your brother still there with you?" Emma's fears had abated greatly when she saw Andrej bring Peter in but they hadn't disappeared completely. Malcolm was still out there. Waiting and watching.

"Yes, he's here," Iris reassured her. "He'll stay the night so you can stop fretting. We're all safe. Now, tell me what you're going to do with the rest of your evening."

"A long soak in a warm bath and then it's bed for me."

"That's it?" Iris' voice had taken on its usual teasing tone. "Isn't there something else you should be doing?"

Emma sighed, she knew where this was going. "Out with it, Iris. I'm tired."

"Yes, I imagine you are. Andrej must be as well."

Emma made a noncommittal sound. It was a shame England couldn't find a way to use Iris as a secret weapon against the Nazis. She never gave up.

"Have you thanked him for saving the day?" Iris persisted. "Properly, I mean?"

Properly? Emma couldn't say that she had. In fact, she'd done everything she could to avoid speaking with him. Their last conversation had been so full of anger that she hadn't wanted to face his wrath. Or his questions. Not tonight. But Iris was right. Andrej had been amazing from the moment he'd learned that Peter had run off. He'd found Peter and returned him safely home. She needed to tell him how deeply, truly grateful she was.

"Not properly, no," she conceded.

"See that you do. And Emma, take that long bath and get properly cleaned up before you go to him. We'll see you in the morning. Late morning." Iris rang off before Emma could say a single word.

ANDREJ TOOK A FRESH SHIRT FROM THE WARDROBE, SLIPPED IT ON AND buttoned it. He towel dried his hair, still wet from his recent bath. Physically he was exhausted, emotionally he was drained, but the warmth in his heart knowing that Peter was safe made it all worth it. He lit a candle and flopped down on his bed, his arms folded behind his head.

He watched the flame flicker and cast shadows against the walls. The comfort and warmth of his bedroom was welcome after the cold rain and wind that he and Peter endured on their journey home. Finding their way in the dark had been tricky. Andrej knew Peter had been well aware of the danger of walking along a dark road when passing motorcars had their lights masked due to blackout regulations.

While still a few miles from the cottage, Peter started to lag. Andrej had offered to carry him but Peter's refusal had been instantaneous. A mile later, he changed his mind and agreed to the offer of help, upon the condition that his sister never learned of it.

A smile stretched across his face. Peter was a wonderful boy. Lily was a sweet girl, and the two of them together hadn't been even a fraction of the trouble he'd been afraid of when he'd moved into Laurel Cottage.

He was a different man now than he'd been just a few short months ago. It was ironic that moving into a small physical space had broadened his world so much. All for the better too. He hadn't a clue how to talk to children then, and now he could at least hold his own in most of their conversations. He'd been terrified the first time Emma had thrust Patrick into his arms. Now he didn't hesitate to take the baby from her when she needed her arms free. He actually rather enjoyed holding the lad, and the way Patrick smiled when he heard Andrej's voice both humbled and amazed him.

Thoughts of Patrick always lead back to Emma. Kind, smart, wonderful Emma. A gentle soul and a practiced liar rolled together into one beautiful woman. Despite his exhaustion, he knew sleep was impossible with all the questions swirling around in his mind.

He cared about Emma far too much to let her face the trouble she was in alone. She was hiding something and her lies today proved that she was too terrified to tell anyone the truth. Whatever her secret was, he was convinced that Peter had learned at least part of it.

Enough. He didn't want to think anymore about it tonight. Tomorrow he would speak with Peter and see if he could get a clue from the boy. As for Emma, he hadn't changed his mind. He was intent upon marrying her so that he could protect her.

He leaned forward to blow out the candle but stopped when someone knocked on his door. Peter, he hoped, had come to confide in him.

"Come in," he called.

The door slowly opened and Andrej's breath caught when he saw Emma in the doorway. Dressed in a pink satin wrapper tied at the waist, her curls hung down around her shoulders. It was the first time he'd seen her hair loose. She was an enchanting vision of loveliness. His heartbeat quickened as he sat up.

"Andrej, I'm sorry to disturb you," she said, her voice more tentative than usual. "I wanted to speak with you for a moment. Were you sleeping?"

"No." Andrej crossed his room and leaned against the door frame. Because he was so much taller than Emma, she was forced to look up at him. The rapid rise and fall of her chest as she breathed surprised him. Was she nervous?

"Come in." He stood back. "Or would you be more comfortable in the sitting room?"

Emma looked past him into his room. As her eyes settled on his bed, he couldn't help but smile at the faint blush that stained her cheeks.

"Perhaps the sitting room is better. But with all that went on today, I didn't think to bring in dry wood for a fire."

"Understandable, it was quite a day. I'll go and have a look."

Andrej had a fire crackling in the grate by the time she returned from the kitchen with a tray in her hands.

"The fire is lovely." She set the tray on the table and sat beside him. "I thought you might be hungry."

Andrej accepted a steaming cup of tea with a grateful smile. "I'm famished." He bit into a sandwich and finished off three more before turning to Emma. "Delicious, thank you."

"They were just sandwiches," Emma shrugged off his compliment.

"I appreciate how difficult it must be to scare up a meal with what we're rationed."

"Let's just say I look forward to a day when the shops actually have shelves full of food like they used to," Emma answered. She sipped her tea and sighed heavily.

"What was that sigh for?"

"I was thinking about Scarlett O'Hara," she smiled ruefully.

"Who?"

Emma turned to him. "Scarlett O'Hara is the lead character is that new American film, *Gone with the Wind*. I take it you haven't seen it?"

"The film with Vivian Leigh and Jimmy Stewart, isn't it?"

"Clark Gable."

"I stand corrected. What made you think of Scarlett just now?"

"Oh, it's silly, really." Emma played with the fringe on the pillow in her lap.

It took every ounce of self-control Andrej had not to reach over and wrap his finger around one of her curls. His rational mind knew there were more pressing matters than American films to discuss, but the sound of Emma's voice was like a siren's call. He'd follow her anywhere the conversation took them just so he could be with her. "Tell me why you were thinking about the film," he encouraged her, pleased when she rewarded him with a smile.

"Atlanta wasn't completely destroyed, even though General Sherman ordered it burned to the ground. The city was rebuilt and eventually became quite prosperous. In a crazy way it gives me hope that we'll be able to say the same thing about London one day."

"Not crazy at all," Andrej said. The BBC Home Service reported relentless bombings night after night. Hope seemed their best defense. "So, this Scarlett, you admired her character, I take it?"

Emma nodded. "She was a survivor. Nothing could keep her down for long. Scarlett did what she had to do to survive, even if she made choices others didn't understand or agree with."

The only sound for several minutes was the fire crackling in the grate. Andrej knew he should find a way to ask Emma the questions that he needed answers to. He owed it to Peter. To Patrick even. But he didn't want to alienate her.

Quite the opposite, his only wish was to draw her close and keep her safe. It amazed him how little anything else mattered to him anymore. He only wanted her. Safe with him. He was so lost in thought that he didn't hear her the first time she called his name. She reached over and gently touched his arm.

"Andrej, there's something I have to tell you." Her eyes were wide, worried.

"No, Emma. Not tonight," he was surprised to hear himself say. He covered her hand with his own. With his thumb he gently caressed her fingers, they were so very tiny compared to his.

"But I need to--"

He reached over and placed two fingers against her lips. He shook his head wordlessly.

Her eyes searched his.

"Tomorrow, Emma. Please."

She gently lowered his hand from her lips but instead of dropping it, she wrapped her fingers through his and cradled their intertwined hands in her lap. "I don't understand. Today you were so angry with me for not telling you...for not..." her voice trailed off.

"Today I was more frightened than I've ever been in my life. And yes, I was angry. But right now Peter is sleeping upstairs and Patrick is safe with Iris." He spoke slowly and softly, sensing her indecision. He didn't want to unnerve her. If she left him now he felt as if his heart would shatter. "Tonight not a single other soul matters, Emma. Just you and I."

Slowly, watching for the slightest resistance from her but sensing none, he gathered Emma into his arms. He buried his face in her curls, savoring the scent of lavender that he'd come to love. He could feel her fingers stroking his hair, their gentle touch driving him nearly mad with desire.

"Andrej, wait." Emma pulled away from him, her eyes filled with uncertainty. "You won't want me after you listen to what I have to say."

"You can't know that." He lifted her hand to his lips and gently kissed it, savoring the softness of her skin.

"I do know it," her voice trembled. "You'll hate me for what I've done."

Andrej cupped her face in his hands and waited until she raised her eyes to meet his.

"My dear Emma, nothing could be further from the truth. I know you need to tell me what has happened, and I want to hear it. I promise I'll help you no matter the consequences. But tomorrow, tonight is for us."

He held his breath, waiting for her response. When finally she nodded her agreement, he stood and pulled her up to stand in front of him. He took a small step back from her but he continued to hold her hands in his.

"I've gone through my entire life alone, Emma, and before I met you that arrangement was acceptable to me. I never aspired to more because I thought I could live with the loneliness. I watched from the outside while others lived their lives." Andrej took a deep breath to fortify his courage. He'd never spoken this honestly to anyone. But Emma wasn't just anyone. She was the woman he loved.

"And then when I met you, everything changed. I didn't plan to, and I didn't want to, but I began to care for you and Patrick, Peter, and Lily. Suddenly, I wanted to hear what you thought and felt. I wanted to be with you all. And when I heard that Peter was missing today I was crazed with worry. I'd never felt fear like that before."

Emma took a step toward him but he shook his head. "Let me finish, please." When she squeezed his hands, Andrej smiled his gratitude.

"Tonight, when we returned to the cottage, I felt like I was coming home. Do you know how many men take this for granted, Emma? All of it, a warm home with a beautiful and intelligent woman, healthy children who are exhausting and delightful all at once. And the baby... when I look at Patrick I see all that is pure and beautiful in this world. This time together has been the greatest gift. Yet I have no right to any of it. Not a moment of it."

"Not true, Andrej," Emma whispered. "You've been nothing but wonderful to all of us. You saved me that first night in London and you saved Peter tonight." She reached up to caress his cheek. "You deserve to be happy. You deserve a family and to be surrounded by people who care about you."

He shook his head. "It will never happen, Emma. And I can accept that. But I'm greedy enough to want one night where I can have it all. I want tonight. I want you."

Andrej watched in agony as Emma closed her eyes. Regret filled him. His selfish choice of words had put her in an untenable position.

"What about what I have to tell you, Andrej? Don't you want to hear what it is that I haven't been honest about?"

"Not tonight, no," he assured her, his refusal emphatic. "Tomorrow, yes. There's nothing you can tell me that will change the way I feel about you. I promise to help you in any way I can. But tonight I want you, Emma."

Agonizing disappointment tore through him as Emma moved past him toward the door. He'd offended her with his blatant proposition. Shame burned through him. He tried to apologize but the words caught in his throat.

"Andrej, look at me."

When he turned, he saw that she'd locked the door. He held out his hand and she came to him without hesitation. His heart filled with tenderness as she stood before him, her fingers playing with his shirt buttons.

"I want to be with you tonight, Andrej."

He heard the desire in her voice. He didn't hear any reluctance, which pleased him even more. "But--"

"Sshh, Andrej--" she interrupted him. "It's your turn to listen to me."

Listen he would, but concentrating while she was slipping the shirt off of his shoulders was virtually impossible. He felt under the spell of a masterful enchantress.

"I'm listening," he assured her, his voice every bit as husky as hers.

"When we make love I want you to promise me that tonight is all you think of. Not a single thought for the mistakes I've made or the problems that await me tomorrow. Promise me."

"I promise," he whispered. He drew Emma into his arms, careful to not crush her too forcibly against his chest.

"I'm not as fragile as you think, Andrej." She leaned into him and gently brushed her lips against his. "I want you."

"You're certain?"

Her answer was to pull his lips to hers in a kiss that was all the permission he needed.

CHAPTER 14

The quiet moments that followed their lovemaking were a balm to his lonely soul. Their fingers intertwined, they lay together, their breathing in harmony the only sound that mattered. Intoxicated with a contentment that had before been unimaginable, Andrej pulled the afghan closer around Emma's shoulders and drew her nearer to him.

"Tell me about your family." She reached up and traced his jawline with her fingertip in a move he found excruciatingly tender. He could hardly find his voice, let alone the words to answer her.

"Please," she whispered. "I want to know more about you."

Andrej lifted one of her curls and twisted it around his finger. Perhaps it was the physical intimacy they had shared, or maybe it was his earlier admission to himself that he loved her, but he felt safe enough to share what few memories he had with her.

"I remember so very little. I was younger than Peter is now when I was sent away. If I have a father, I don't remember anything about him, nor brothers and sisters. Perhaps I was an only child."

"Your mother?" Emma coaxed, her voice low and gentle.

He hesitated. The thought of his mother was always the most

painful part of remembering. "I'm never sure what I actually remember and what my mind has made up."

"Tell me."

And so he did. He started with the only memory he could clearly recall. He and his mother were on a train, but from where they'd journeyed, he couldn't say. He remembered the way the countryside passed in a blur, also the way the train cars gently rocked as they sped along. His mother had worn a wool coat, bottle green he remembered, with a silk scarf. He closed his eyes and tried to recall more. Scuffed, worn shoes, he could see those. Had she carried a handbag? No, he couldn't recall one, but she had clutched a white handkerchief tightly in her hand.

"Perhaps she was crying," Emma suggested when he stopped speaking.

Crying? Andrej had never considered that. Truthfully, his thoughts were usually focused on what he felt that day. He'd given little thought to what his mother might have felt. His memories centered around a little boy who started off on an adventure with his mother. The day had ended with a bewildering goodbye and whispered words that haunted him for decades. *You don't belong with our family, Andrej.*

After he shared the same words with Emma, the first time he'd ever said them aloud, he waited for her response. As he held his breath, he realized how much her reaction mattered to him. In Emma, he wished for redemption. He wished for permission to feel a part of something other than his lonely world.

But even if she never uttered a word, it wouldn't matter. The fact she cared enough to let him touch her so intimately, and the way she wanted to know more about him, was all that he needed to feel, for however brief a time, that he was worthy of being cared about. She would never love him. He knew and accepted that. But, in some fashion, she cared. He tightened his hold on her. This time together was precious.

"Do you know what I think?" Emma asked.

He ran his fingers through her curls. He couldn't take his eyes from her lips, their softness tantalized him. Not kissing her felt a cruel torture. "Tell me."

"I think that your mother saw your talent as something far greater than she alone could manage." Emma leaned in to brush her lips against his in the softest of kisses. "What you thought of as a rejection, I see as a sacrifice she made on your behalf. She gave her son to people who could honor his talent in a way she couldn't. She wasn't giving you away. She was trying to give you the world."

"Why didn't she tell me that?"

"Oh, Andrej," Emma propped herself up on her elbow. "Don't you see that the greatest gift of love that your mother could have given you was the freedom to develop your talent? Look at all that she gave you by taking you to people who could nurture your abilities. Iris told me that you're revered in international circles as one of the greatest classical pianists of our time. All that you've done, all the places you've gone, and the joy you've brought to people through your music, it was because your mother loved you enough to make such a sacrifice ."

"Sacrifice," he repeated the word slowly, as if doing so would help him believe what Emma seemed so very convinced of. It wasn't an easy idea to accept. The greatest gift his mother could have given him was to keep her with him and to love him fiercely, the way Emma did Patrick.

"She made an unbearably painful choice, Andrej. Can't you see it?" Emma demanded. "She let you go so that you would have all that you deserved, all that she wanted you to have. I can't believe that for all of these years you've resented your mother instead of being grateful to her."

"You make it sound so simple," he protested. "It isn't."

"Of course, it isn't. You can't know if what she did for you was for the best or not. I imagine your mother has lain awake many nights wondering the same thing. Have you ever tried to contact her?"

He shook his head. "No, I didn't want to hear that she had forgotten me. Nor did I wish to be sent away again." His eyes met hers. The tenderness in her gaze was almost unbearable.

"We don't have to talk about it now," she reassured him. She drew him to her, his head resting on her chest. She stroked his hair as they lay together in silence.

This feeling of being connected, of excitement and pleasure, of trust and surrender, he was able to finally understand, was what it felt like to love.

EVER SO SLOWLY, SO AS NOT TO AWAKEN ANDREJ, EMMA SLIPPED OUT OF his arms. A rush of cold air hit her as she left the warm protection of his embrace. She breathed a sigh of relief when he didn't stir. The fire that provided them with warmth last night was now only a pile of cold ashes.

After a quick search, Emma found her dressing gown and wrapper. She quickly dressed and then surveyed the room. The disarray was proof of the previous night's passion. A contented smile played across her lips. A quiet gratitude for her connection with Andrej warmed her heart. She glanced at the clock on the mantle. There was no time for this sort of thinking now. She needed to get upstairs before the children awoke.

As quietly as she was able, she restored the room to its previous state. When the last pillow was picked up off the floor, Emma crept over to look down at Andrej one last time. She didn't know when, or if, she would ever have the chance again to watch him sleep.

Missing the warmth and safety of his embrace, she wrapped her arms around her waist. Making love with Andrej had felt so natural. She couldn't help but smile at the memory of his tender touch. Who could ever have believed that a man so large could be capable of such gentleness? More to the point, she couldn't believe that she'd given of herself so freely. But she didn't regret it. Last night was now her cherished memory and no one could take it away from her. For that, she was desperately grateful.

She looked around one last time. The room looked just as it had last night. It was she who had changed. She pulled back the blackout curtains. It wouldn't be long before the sun would stream into the room and wake Andrej. She didn't want him to see her until she was able to get her emotions in check. The way he'd looked into her eyes last night made her feel like he could see into her soul.

For the first time since she'd discovered her cousin's lifeless body, she felt a tiny glimmer of hope. Her future was devoted to protecting Patrick. After last night, she dared to hope there would be room for Andrej in her life as well.

A quick look into Peter and Lily's room reassured her they were still asleep. She closed her bedroom door and quickly bathed and dressed. The room felt empty without Patrick and she was anxious to see him again. To have both Peter and Patrick back at home would be a blessing. The last twenty-four hours had been a whirlwind of emotions, starting with panic and fear and now...hope.

Emma closed her wardrobe doors and straightened Patrick's cot. She pulled at her duvet and smoothed it out, quietly singing as she did so. How on earth was she going to keep this silly grin off of her face? She knew Iris would know what had happened the moment she saw Emma, and then she would be bombarded with questions. Questions she wasn't going to answer. Last night's lovemaking, every delicious moment of it, was between she and Andrej alone.

From the corner of her eye, Emma saw that the bed skirt wasn't straight. Odd, she hadn't slept in the bedroom and no one should have been in the room. As she bent down to adjust the bedding, an uneasy sensation came over her.

Dropping down to her knees, she peered up under the mattress. Her heart caught in her throat and she barely kept from crying out. The envelope she had hidden under the mattress had been moved. She took it out and slid the letters out onto the carpet. They had obviously been looked through. She'd taken great care to fold them in a particular manner when she last put them away, but now they were completely out of order. Her hands trembled as she sorted through them, quickly counting them.

They were all there. But who had gone through them? Surely the children hadn't touched her things? No, of course not. Why would they? And even if they did find the letters they wouldn't be able to read them. They were all in German. No one in the house spoke German.

Except for Andrej.

Andrej, the man she had given herself to so freely last night, had betrayed her. Used her. Played her for a fool. That she could be so foolish, so unwitting, and so insanely stupid made her feel ill. It couldn't be true. She didn't want to believe it but a glance down at the letters was all the proof she needed. There could be no other explanation.

But why? Had last night been a trick? She had gone to see Andrej on her own, he hadn't come to her. Had he just been waiting for an opportunity to take advantage of her? Questions swirled round her mind. What would he stand to gain by sleeping with her? Had everything he told her simply been a lie? A story meant to draw her in and elicit her sympathy?

She covered her face with her hands and rocked back and forth. A furious blush covered her cheeks. She felt such an idiot. A cheap, common fool.

In agonizingly slow motion, her mind's eye watched as it all fell into place. She hadn't confided in Andrej about the baby last night, but she'd planned to do so today. He knew that too, she'd told him she would. So why had he made love to her?

A deep burning shame stole over her. Andrej made love to her so she would lower her guard and confess that Patrick wasn't her son. If that happened it would no longer be her word against Malcolm's if he accused her of kidnapping. There would be a witness who could testify against her.

Why would Andrej want to hurt her by taking Patrick from her? He knew she loved the baby more than her own life. There could only be one answer.

Andrej was working for Malcolm.

"A SPECIAL OCCASION, SIR?"

Andrej glanced up at the waiter and nodded. "Thank you." He held up his hand to signal that his water glass was full. He wished the glass was full of wine rather than water, but this was a small family owned restaurant in Brighton and not the Savoy.

"A very special occasion," Peter piped up when Andrej didn't directly answer the waiter's question. "Mr. Van der Hoosen is going to get engaged tonight."

"Please accept my wishes for a most happy marriage." The elderly waiter motioned toward the two empty place settings. "Would you care to order before your party arrives, Sir?"

Andrej opened his mouth to speak but this time it was Lily who interrupted.

"At least we hope there will be an engagement tonight," she explained to the waiter. "Aunt Emma hasn't been asked properly yet, has she, Mr. Van der Hoosen?"

"That's what this evening is for," Peter interjected. "We're just waiting for Aunt Emma and her friend to arrive now."

Andrej couldn't help but smile as the waiter continued to back away whilst the children chattered on. He had to marvel at Peter's resilience. Yesterday had been an incredible ordeal for the boy, and just this morning Peter sat and spun a yarn for the adults about chasing rabbits, accidentally speaking with the prisoner about the weather, and then getting lost in the woods. Not a word of which any of them believed, but they had at least managed to extract a promise that he wouldn't leave the cottage again without permission from an adult.

He planned to speak with Peter at length the next morning. The boy knew something and Andrej wanted to know what it was.

He'd watched Emma closely during the telling of Peter's tale. She'd refused to meet his eye all the while the lad spoke. Was this avoidance because she was embarrassed about their shared intimacy the previous evening? He hoped not. Whatever it was, he hadn't pressed her for an explanation. She'd accepted his invitation to dine out that night in Brighton, which was all he wanted from her. That she'd asked to bring a friend had only slightly surprised him. Perhaps she wanted to repay Iris for taking care of Patrick and thought an evening out would be a treat.

He glanced at his watch. Doubtless it had taken them longer than they planned to scare up an unwitting soul to watch Iris' brood.

Including Peter and Lily had been a last minute decision but they'd been delighted at the offer of a grown-up evening out. He hoped Emma wouldn't mind. Because restaurants weren't restricted by rations, he thought it would be a treat for the children to have a proper meal and eat until they were full.

It wouldn't be the most romantic proposal imaginable with Peter, Lily, and Iris along, but this marriage wasn't about offering Emma romance. It was about offering her legal protection.

Lost in thought, Andrej started when Peter spoke.

"Shall we go over what you're going to say again, Sir?" Peter asked.

"No, no, Peter," Lily interjected, a note of panic in her voice.

"What's wrong, Lily?" Andrej asked.

"I know what she's going to say," Peter grumbled.

"Then let's let her say it," Andrej suggested.

"You sound just like you're a proper father when you talk like that," Peter said, more than a hint of approval in his tone. "Which is good if you're going to become Patrick's father."

Patrick's father. Andrej felt a fleeting stab of regret. For a second the idea resonated within his heart but just as quickly it was gone. Patrick needed to be with his real family. Andrej was going to do whatever necessary to see that it happened. Emma was going to hate him. He glanced toward the doorway, searching those waiting to be seated. Emma and Iris were nowhere in sight. He checked his watch again.

"Don't worry," Lily reassured him. "She'll be here. Now let's get back to what you're supposed to say."

"Supposed to say?" He repeated, suddenly very unsure. Proposing to Emma in public with others present had seemed a good idea this morning. Now, he wasn't so certain.

Lily sighed deeply. "Mr. Van der Hoosen, please focus. This is important. You are going to ask Aunt Emma to marry you so you need to find just the right words."

"Such as?"

Peter didn't hide his amusement. "Just make something up for him to memorize, Lily."

Lily scoffed at her brother's suggestion. "Hush, Peter. This isn't the time to memorize anything. Mr. Van der Hoosen needs to pull the words from his heart." She turned to face Andrej. "I think you should tell Aunt Emma why you love her, why you think she's special, and why you want to spend the rest of your life with her."

The rest of his life? Uneasiness settled in the pit of Andrej's stomach. Now he was the liar. His words would propose marriage but his intent was to propose a way out of trouble. Not that it wouldn't be a dream come true to spend the rest of his life with Emma. What man could ask for more? She was beautiful, kind, intelligent, generous, and passionate. She was also in terrible trouble. "I'm not sure this is such a good idea, Lily," Andrej hedged. "Perhaps this isn't the time or place tonight--"

"Too late," Peter interrupted. "I see Aunt Emma now." He half stood from his chair and craned his neck toward the restaurant entrance. He groaned. "It's Aunt Emma alright, with her chump…I mean chum, in tow."

Andrej and Lily both turned to look.

Emma stood in the doorway, resplendent in a cream silk dress he hadn't seen her wear before. A matching ribbon was threaded through her curls and a string of delicate pearls were around her neck. Stuart, wearing a suit and tie, stood beside her.

"Oh, doesn't she look enchanting?" Lily cried.

"That she does." Andrej stood and motioned for them to join their table. Emma did look lovely. She looked like a woman with not a care in the world, but he knew better.

"I don't know why she had to drag him along," Peter grumbled.

Andrej turned, surprised. "You don't care for Lieutenant Tollison?"

Peter shrugged. "He's a decent enough chap, I suppose, just not terribly bright."

"Don't be unkind, Peter," Lily scolded. "Although I'll agree that it certainly is bad timing for him to be here." She settled her napkin on her lap and folded her hands in front of her. "Let's at least hope he remains quiet during the proposal."

Andrej was saved from having to come up with a response by Emma and Stuart's arrival at the table. He stood and shook the younger man's right hand, the fact that Stuart's left hand lingered possessively at the small of Emma's back didn't escape his notice. He frowned.

"Something wrong, Sir?" Stuart asked.

"No," Andrej answered, sounding curt even to his ears. He really couldn't blame the lad. He'd show the same possessiveness toward Emma if he were in Stuart's place.

"Sit here between us, Lieutenant." Lily patted the empty chair between herself and Peter.

The children had quickly moved a seat apart in an effort to separate Emma and Stuart. Andrej smiled to convey his gratitude to his little allies. He waited until Emma was seated to speak to her. "You look beautiful this evening, Emma."

"Doesn't she?" Stuart agreed, his smile wide. "Makes a chap proud to have such a lovely lady on his arm."

"Thank you for inviting us, Andrej," Emma said, her words uncharacteristically stiff. Her gaze softened when she looked at the children. "You two look rather spiffy."

"Wasn't it kind of Mr. Van der Hoosen to invite us along?" Lily said.

"Indeed."

Andrej searched Emma's face for a clue to what she was feeling. Shyness he could understand after last night. It had been their first time being intimate. But something told him this wasn't what accounted for Emma's strange behavior. Her tightly controlled words and refusal to look at him weren't a sign of bashfulness, but anger. What had he done?

After the waiter left with their order, an awkward silence descended over the table. Andrej looked to Peter and Lily for guidance. Peter merely shrugged. Lily nodded her encouragement. Andrej groaned inwardly. What on earth had possessed him to do this in a public place?

He longed to be alone with Emma. Their shared connection that had warmed his heart last night was gone, replaced by an uncomfortable, confusing silence. He cleared his throat.

"Are you all right, old chap?" Stuart asked.

Old chap. Andrej resisted the urge to frown. What was it about Stuart that made him feel an old, wobbly third wheel? To keep the evening from becoming a total fiasco he needed to do something. He took a deep breath and plunged in.

"Emma, I hope you know how very much I have appreciated the opportunity to work beside you these last months." He paused. "This time with you has been truly the greatest experience of my life."

Emma continued to look at her hands, which he could see were clearly trembling.

An overwhelming tenderness rose in Andrej's chest, making it difficult for him to speak. He remembered the look of fear in Emma's eye when he found her in London being harassed by soldiers. Her determination to reach the train station that night shone in her eyes when she had defiantly refused to seek shelter. He thought of all the other times she had looked into his eyes and smiled so readily. Her laughter, her kindness…it was always in her eyes. He desperately wished she would look at him now.

He reached out to cover her hands with one of his but she dropped her hands into her lap.

"I think the world of you, Emma. I care deeply for you and Patrick and there is nothing that I want more than to spend the rest of my life with you both." As the words came unbidden to his lips, Andrej knew he spoke the truth. His truth. He'd give everything he had to marry Emma. But he wanted her forever. Not just temporarily, and not just to help her out of trouble. He wanted it all, every moment of the rest of their lives.

He wasn't going to take no for an answer. She cared for him. He knew she did, at least in some small way. Ignoring the curious restaurant patrons, Stuart's confused look, and the children's intent gaze, Andrej stood and moved his chair aside. He dropped down on one knee beside Emma's chair and lifted her chin so that she was forced to meet his eyes.

"I love you, Emma," he said tenderly, his words gentle and coaxing. "Will you marry me?"

"I can't." Her eyes filled with tears.

"You can." He kissed both of her hands in turn. "I promise you no matter what happens I will never leave you."

Emma shook her head. "No, Andrej, you don't understand. I can't marry you."

"Emma, please don't turn me away without thinking about it carefully. At least hear me out. I know you're frightened but we can face anything if we're together."

Stuart came to stand behind Emma's chair. He looked down at Andrej. "She can't marry you, Sir. We got engaged a few hours ago." He grinned. "By this time tomorrow, Emma will be my wife."

CHAPTER 15

"*I* assume this isn't how you envisioned spending the night before your wedding," Andrej said as he closed the door to the cellar behind them.

Emma was grateful for the dark that hid her flushed expression. From the moment Stuart blurted out the truth about their betrothal, she couldn't make herself meet Andrej's gaze. But now, not an hour later, Stuart was gone and Andrej was close enough to reach out and gather her into his arms if he so wanted.

"Ah, here it is," Andrej said as he reached out and pulled a chain. A small bulb provided just enough light to create shadows.

Emma surveyed the cramped cellar that was going to serve as their makeshift shelter for the night. She shifted uneasily as Peter and Lily began to explore their surroundings.

"I hate the Germans," Emma seethed. "I absolutely detest them. Every last one of them. I'd happily strangle a Nazi with my bare hands right now if I could find one."

"Be that as it may," Andrej's voice was low enough only she could hear him, "let us try not to frighten the children."

"I would never intentionally frighten them." Annoyed by Andrej's apparent calmness in the storm of her own anger at his betrayal,

Emma took a step away from him. The heel of her shoe caught on a rope and she pitched forward. A small cry escaped her lips as Andrej reached out and broke her fall by pulling her back against him.

"You have every right to be angry, Emma, but not with me," Andrej said. "Your pre-wedding celebration was rudely interrupted by the Luftwaffe, not me."

Emma stumbled slightly as Andrej abruptly let go of her. She squared her shoulders and smoothed her dress. His words were true enough. He wasn't responsible for the air raid wardens call to evacuate the restaurant. But he was responsible for betraying her, and she had no idea how she was going to bear being in such small quarters until the all-clear call came.

"Will everyone call you Mrs. Tollison after tomorrow, Aunt Emma?" Lily called from across the cellar where she and Peter were looking around.

"Yes, I suppose they will." She shot Andrej a pointed look over her shoulder. "But not all that much has changed really."

"That might be news to Lieutenant Tollison," Peter chimed in. "At dinner he went on and on about being a married man and his new responsibilities."

Andrej chuckled. Emma frowned.

This conversation didn't need to go any further. She tried to redirect Peter's attention away from the awkward meal they had all just shared. Half a meal, really, because a telephone message had recalled Stuart to the airfield. He'd told them that radar reports showed a great deal of incoming aircraft. Rather than risk returning to the cottage, Andrej had accepted the restaurant owner's offer of the cellar to wait the air raid out. She'd had no real choice but to bring the children down to safety.

"Have you found any cots?" she asked.

"Yes, two." Peter dragged them out from where they were stored.

She stood aside and watched as Andrej helped the children set them up against the wall.

"I've found pillows and blankets," Lily called. "Peter and I can share one cot. You and Mr. Van der Hoosen can..." her voice trailed off.

"Deuced awkward," Peter commented as he looked between the two adults.

Emma tried to ignore Andrej's amused smirk. "You two just go ahead and set those up for yourselves. Mr. Van der Hoosen and I will sit somewhere else." She looked around the dimly lit cellar but the boxes and crates piled up to the ceiling left little obvious place to wait. "I doubt any of us will be able to sleep tonight but you might as well be comfortable."

"I am most certainly going to sleep," Peter said. "If the restaurant gets bombed and crushes us, I'd much prefer to be asleep while it happens."

"That's quite enough of that talk, young man," Andrej corrected him. "I think we've had quite enough excitement for the evening as it were. Don't you agree, Emma?"

Ignoring his question, Emma turned toward the children. "There will be no falling buildings tonight so let's not speak about like that, Peter. I'm more worried that you're going to miss a good night's sleep than anything else."

She placed one pillow at each end of the cot and motioned for the children to lie down. Once they did she spread a blanket over them and kissed the top of their heads. "There now, I've put your gas masks by your shoes. You go to sleep and I'll be right here."

"With Mr. Van der Hoosen?" Peter asked.

The memory of their shared passion last night flashed through her mind. Everything had seemed so different then. Of course, that was before she found out that Andrej was a lying snake who worked for Malcolm. "Yes, with Mr. Van der Hoosen."

"Aunt Emma?"

"One last question, Peter, and that's all for tonight."

"Are the Americans going to come and help us fight?"

The angst in his young voice caused Emma's heart to ache.

Andrej crouched down beside the children's cot. "In the last war the Americans and the Canadians came to help, Peter, and they'll come again. And when it's all over there will be grand celebrations. That much I can promise you." He ruffled Peter's hair, then Lily's, and stood. "You'll be able to tell everyone how incredibly brave you and your sister were during all of this."

The drone of aircraft overhead grew so loud they had to wait for it to pass before anyone could speak again.

"I hate the sound of planes," Lily said once the sound grew fainter.

"In that plane, Lily, are some very brave British airmen who are going to keep us safe tonight," Andrej told her. "Does that make it easier to hear when you think of it that way?"

Emma watched as Lily nodded and then yawned. Within moments the children were both asleep. She marveled at how quickly they could fall asleep in unfamiliar surroundings.

She looked for a place to sit. There was nowhere but the dusty stairs they'd just come down. The rough wooden planks looked uncomfortable and filthy.

"Wait," Andrej caught her arm as she headed towards the steps. "Go sit on the cot while I turn off the light."

Emma hesitated. She didn't know which way to turn, where to sit, and who to trust. She obviously couldn't trust her own judgment. Not when it came to Andrej. She'd made love with him. She'd allowed him to hold her in his arms, completely unaware of his duplicity. Worst of all, she'd almost told him the truth about Patrick.

"Go on, Emma," Andrej gave her a gentle nudge in the direction of the cot. "Don't fall apart on me now."

She stared back. He was right. Falling apart, caving in, or losing her way was simply not an option. Patrick needed her. She took a deep breath. Her only real choice was to get as far away from Andrej as possible. Tomorrow. Tonight she was stuck with him. She sat stiffly on the edge of the cot and waited while Andrej turned off the light. The cot groaned beneath his weight when he sat beside her. She inched away.

A startled cry escaped her lips when Andrej slid his arm around her waist and drew her back beside him. "Sshhh...you're fine," he assured her, his voice just above a whisper. "Let's not wake the children."

"Don't tell me how to handle the children," she snapped.

Her voice sounded waspish. She could hear it clearly but she was an absolute mess of emotions. Desperately, she wished to be anywhere else in the world but stuck in a small restaurant cellar with Andrej.

The only way this evening could have turned out worse was if Malcolm was beside her. Malcolm. Andrej. How much difference was there really between the two of them?

God help her, but she was a fool. And she'd made a narrow escape from sharing the truth with Andrej. Asking Stuart to marry her, and insisting that it be that next day, had seemed, at the moment, a way to put a measure of protection between herself and Malcolm. The decision had been impetuous and already it seemed futile. In her heart she knew that Stuart, no matter how well-meaning, was no match for Malcolm.

She was trapped, and not just for the duration of tonight's air raid. Tears pricked at the back of her eyes but she wouldn't give them the satisfaction of letting them fall. She sat stiffly beside Andrej, not bothering to try to move. There was nowhere to go.

"Emma."

She ignored him.

"We need to talk." Andrej's voice was low but insistent.

He could rot before she'd waste her breath answering him.

"We need to talk about Patrick," he persisted. "Damn it Emma, this trouble you're in isn't going to go away simply because you want it to."

She bit her tongue to keep her uncharitable response to herself.

"Tollison's a fine lad but he's not the help you need now. I am."

Emma clenched her fists. The man had nerve speaking to her like he wanted to help when, in truth, he was looking for just the right angle to stick a knife in her back.

"You can explain your hasty engagement to me later," he continued. "Right now it's time for you to tell me what you wanted to say last night. Before I stopped you, before we--"

"Not another word," she interrupted him before he went any further. She couldn't bear to hear him speak about last night like it was nothing. To her, it had been something. Which now made her feel all the more stupid. And angry. "Don't you dare."

"We can talk about something else, like Patrick's father. Tell me who he is and why you're terrified of him."

Silence was all he was going to get from her.

"I can help you, Emma," he urged.

Emma twisted around toward him. It was too dark to see him. How she wished there was enough light for him to see the anger she knew was blazing in her eyes.

"I know what you want, Andrej, and it's not to help Patrick. Or me." She took a deep, steadying breath. It was foolish to divulge what she knew about him but she couldn't stop herself. Damn Andrej and damn Malcolm. "I know who you are," she spat out, the rage in her voice palpable. "I know that you want to take Patrick from me and I know you work for Malcolm. You've lied to me over and over again."

"What are you talking about?"

She stiffened when his arm tightened around her waist. She tried to push it away but he only tightened his hold. "Don't treat me like I'm stupid."

"For the love of God, Emma, get a hold of yourself," Andrej scolded her. "You're going to wake the children if you don't lower your voice. "

Emma knew he was right. The children had been through enough for one night. They'd be better off asleep rather than listening to a row.

"We're talking at cross-purposes here. Let's start again. Tell me where this anger is coming from."

It didn't escape her notice that his voice was low and controlled, as if he were talking to the village idiot. Which, she could argue, she'd been. The night she'd met Andrej in London had been a set-up. Not divine intervention as she'd so naively thought. She felt so unbearably stupid.

"Who is Malcolm?" Andrej's voice interrupted her thoughts.

"Oh, please, don't act like you don't know."

He let out an exasperated sigh. "I tell you, I don't know. I don't want to see anything or anyone hurt either you or Patrick. Let me help you."

Emma's heart twisted in her chest. She'd never spent this much time away from the baby. It hurt.

"I'm not going to give up asking until you tell me the trouble that you're in, Emma." He waited several moments before he spoke again. "I'm afraid for you."

Afraid for her? Ah, so he did know Malcolm and the extent of his evil ways.

"You can tell me about this Malcolm or not, Emma. It's your choice. But either way I'm going to get the information somehow. Perhaps Laura will be able to tell me--"

The whistle of a rocket cut off his words, giving them only a moment's warning before the ground shook from the bomb's impact. The strength of its reverberations meant the hit had been close. She pressed her palms into her forehead. Sometimes it was hard not to give into panic, and this was one of those moments. "Leave Laura alone," she warned Andrej. "She's not a part of this at all."

"A part of what?" Andrej demanded. "Curse it, Emma, you're acting mad. What on earth has happened to you since last night to make you so hostile?"

Emma shot to her feet. "What has happened to me? My God, Andrej, you've got unbelievable cheek." She took several tentative steps away from him. It was too dark to see where she was going but she was desperate to put distance between them. "Fine, I'll say it out loud but we both know what you've done."

Andrej was at her side before she finished speaking. He took a hold of her shoulders. "Say it then. Whatever it is that you are so angry about, just tell me."

Emma tried to pull away but Andrej had too firm a hold on her. She choked back a sob. Last night he had been so gentle, so kind, and she'd felt so safe. *Last night he made a fool of you. Last night he slept with you to get information to hurt Patrick.*

None too gently, he led her back to the cot. "Sit down." He spoke again when she sat. "I'm out of patience with your refusal to answer my questions."

The wail of a passing ambulance siren in the street above added to the somber atmosphere. If Brighton was undergoing a pounding from the Luftwaffe, Emma shuddered to think what was happening in London tonight. The nightly bombings there had been merciless for months now, was that the German's plan for the south of England now?

"I can't force you to tell me anything, Emma, but that isn't going to stop me from discovering what trouble you're in."

"What are you going to do, Andrej? Look under my bed again for a fresh batch of letters?" Emma couldn't keep the sarcasm out of her voice.

"Under your bed? You're not making any sense." Andrej sounded genuinely confused.

What a load of rubbish. "Spare me the innocent act. This morning, when I went upstairs, it was obvious that you found Malcolm's letters."

"I wish I knew who this Malcolm person is," Andrej said.

"Malcolm...the man you work for...the scum who sent you to discover where I was hiding the damning information I have on him," she cried. "Is any of this sounding familiar yet, Andrej?"

"My God, Emma, you're confusing the hell out of me. I have no idea what you're talking about. How many times do I have to tell you that? I have never been in your room and I have not, nor ever would, touch any of your things."

"Liar." Emma heard the rage seeping back into her words. "Who else would be going through my things? Who else speaks fluent German and could read the letters? If it wasn't you, then who was it?"

"It was me, Aunt Emma."

She froze. A deafening silence filled the cellar.

"Peter," Andrej said, "Listen to me carefully before you say another word. This is a serious adult matter we're discussing. I need to know that every word you are about to speak is the exact truth. Do you understand me?"

"Yes, Sir."

"Is Lily awake?" Emma asked.

"I am, Aunt Emma, but I'm frightened."

"Everything will be fine," she lied. She clasped her hands together to stop them from shaking. "We're safe and nothing bad is going to happen. We just have to sort this out."

"Peter," Andrej said. "I think you owe us an explanation."

"Yes, I know I do. I'm sorry, Aunt Emma, but it wasn't Mr. Van der Hoosen who looked at your letters. It was me."

"But why, Peter?" A sickening regret began to spread through her. She'd accused Andrej when it was Peter who had gone through Malcolm's letters. Was there no end to her foolishness?

"Are you certain you really want to know?" Peter asked. "The truth?"

"Stop hedging," Andrej answered for them both. "Start talking, Peter. And mind you don't fabricate a single word this time. This morning we let you get away with your story about chasing rabbits into the woods, but right now you need to be honest about what you've done. Patrick's safety depends on you."

"I understand, Sir." Peter cleared his throat. "It all started when I was up in the tree. I was dangling from a high limb one morning when I overheard Aunt Emma talking to Patrick about his mother. His real mother."

Emma gasped. Andrej laid his hand on her arm. She understood what he was trying to tell her. Peter would be far more forthcoming if she remained silent.

"Go on," Andrej prompted him.

"I was confused but I didn't want to ask Aunt Emma what she meant so I came to you, Sir." Peter hesitated. "But you didn't want to listen to me and you made it clear I should stay out of Aunt Emma's business. I couldn't, though, because I started to worry about her."

"Worried in what way, son?" Andrej asked.

"Well, I mean, it's obvious, isn't it? Patrick's real mum must be looking for him. If she can't find him then she'd go round to the police to ask for help. Once the police are involved...well, I figured it couldn't look good for Aunt Emma. People who steal babies get into a frightful amount of trouble."

Emma couldn't keep quiet any longer. Whatever Peter had done wrong, he didn't deserve to worry like this. "Peter, I didn't steal Patrick from anyone. He's not my son, he's my cousin."

"So who is Patrick's mother?"

"She was my cousin, Patricia." Emma choked over the word *was*.

"Emma isn't the one who is answering questions right now, Peter. You are."

Andrej reached over and took hold of Emma's hand. She was grateful for his steady warmth as she listened to him question Peter about the letters. She struggled to concentrate, however, as she realized how horribly she'd misjudged Andrej. He hadn't betrayed her. She'd made love with him and then immediately afterward believed the worst of him.

"Aunt Emma, will you ever forgive me?" Peter asked, his voice anxious. "Please, say you will. I know I was wrong, but I was frightened that you were in terrible trouble."

"Oh, Peter, of course, I accept your apology. But please tell me that you understand everything Mr. Van der Hoosen has just told you about how serious this situation is."

"I do, really I do. I promise I won't do anything at all without asking either of you first."

"That's not good enough, Peter," Andrej said. "You need to promise to not do anything at all. You need to forget what you've seen and heard. I cannot overstate how important it is for Emma and Patrick's safety that you are silent about this matter."

Peter immediately agreed, his manner unquestionably contrite. They sat in silence for what felt like interminable time, the only sound that of aircraft overhead.

"Do you think they're asleep?" Andrej whispered.

"They are. I don't know how, but they are."

His voice sounded amazingly level, calm, and caring. His generosity made her feel all the worse. She'd accused him of deceit and treachery when he'd never been anything but kind to her. Emma's throat tightened. No one, in fact, had ever been more compassionate toward her than Andrej had.

"Andrej, will you ever forgive me?" Emma held her breath as she waited for him to say something, anything, to ease her guilt.

Instead of answering, he drew her closer. His fingers caressed her cheek as his lips sought hers in a kiss so tender that her heart ached all the more. He leaned his forehead against hers for a long moment before pulling away.

"Help me understand, Emma," he said. "Malcolm is Patrick's father?"

"Yes," she forced herself to say.

"And you have the letters to use against Malcolm if he tries to take Patrick away from you. Is that right?"

"Yes, that's exactly right."

"Malcolm will hang for treason if those letters are turned over to the authorities, you are correct," he said. "But have you thought about what the police will do when they learn you withheld this information back for your own use?"

"Of course, I have," she forced herself to say. "But I was desperate to keep Patrick safe. I don't care what happens to me as long as it means he's safe from Malcolm."

Andrej drew her into his embrace and rocked her soothingly. Within the safety of his arms, she clung to him as if he were a lifeline.

"I'm afraid," she confessed.

"You should be." He dropped a kiss onto her forehead. "I will keep you and Patrick safe, but you need to trust me."

"I do." Her words came easily, directly from her heart. But they were also terribly ironic considering that they were the same words she was meant to utter at her wedding to Stuart the next day. "I do trust you."

"Then give me the letters."

CHAPTER 16

*E*mma was halfway up the stairs when she heard the front door knocker. She hesitated. It was probably Stuart. She felt a fleeting moment of panic. She'd been so wrapped up in worry over Malcolm that she'd not yet decided what to say when she saw him. After a long night waiting out the air raid, they'd arrived back at the cottage early this morning. She'd spent the day working up at the Manor but Stuart hadn't once dropped by to see her. This she'd attributed to the likelihood he was asleep after an exhausting night flying. She knew he had to have been disappointed that they were unable to keep their appointment at the registrar's office. However unprepared she was to see him now, leaving him on the door step wasn't an option. She smoothed back her hair, straightened her skirt, and pulled open the front door.

Her eyes widened in surprise. It wasn't Stuart. "Good evening, Sir."

Wing Commander Blythe nodded and removed his hat. "Emma."

"Come in, please." She ushered him in and shut the door behind him. "Andrej is in the sitting room. Please go on through." She turned towards the staircase.

"Wait, Emma. I need to speak with both you and Andrej."

The gravity in his voice surprised Emma but she wasn't to be deterred. Getting the letters safely into Andrej's hands was more important than anything else could possibly be.

"I'm sorry, Sir, but I've something extremely important to see to just now. Would you please brief Andrej without me? He'll explain everything to me later."

"No. I've come with news of Stuart."

A cold feeling of dread wrapped itself around Emma's throat, rendering her unable to ask the question she knew she needed to.

He led her gently into the sitting room. Emma sank onto the sofa.

Andrej put aside his book when they entered the room. "Wing Commander," he acknowledged the other man as he crossed to Emma's side. He sat beside her and took her trembling hands in his. "What has happened?"

"It's Stuart." Emma was unable to say anything more.

"What of him?" Andrej demanded. "He was on a flying mission tonight, yes?"

W.C. Blythe cleared his throat. "Yes, Flight Lieutenant Tollison completed his mission and returned safely to the airfield over an hour ago."

"Oh, thank God." Emma's heart was still racing. She took several deep steadying breaths. "Why have you come? Did Stuart send a message for me?"

"No, not exactly." The Wing Commander shifted uncomfortably from one leg to the other.

"Good heavens, Blythe, say what you have to say," Andrej ordered him. "You're frightening Emma."

"Yes, of course. My apologies, Emma." He came and sat on the other side of her. He placed a hand on her shoulder. "Tollison and his flight partner did return safely from a successful mission. Both of them entered the hangar to file a mission report but Tollison returned to the plane after a flight mechanic reported seeing someone they couldn't identify approach the Spitfire."

Emma's throat constricted. "Go on," she forced herself to say.

"It all happened so fast. The aircraft turned into a ball of flames.

We haven't yet been able to determine exactly what caused the explosion."

"Where is Stuart now?" Andrej asked.

Emma held her breath. *Please God, please let him be unharmed.* But the look on the Wing Commander's face told her that her hopes were futile. Her thoughts of Stuart had been few and far between during the day. Instead she had been consumed with thoughts of Patrick, Malcolm, herself. And Andrej.

Not Stuart.

"Is he--" Emma couldn't bring herself to finish the question.

"He's been very badly burned." Blythe stood and began to pace the sitting room.

Emma hardly recognized the agitated man before her.

"Stuart's alive. But you must understand how grave his injuries are. He's been moved to the Royal Sussex County Hospital. I spoke to the attending consultant just before I came here."

Emma felt the gentle, steadying presence of Andrej's hand on her back as she struggled to focus on the words Wing Commander Blythe spoke.

"Tell us what the consultant said," Andrej said.

"Stuart has suffered extensive burns over much of his body. The physician I spoke with is stunned that he even survived the blast. He's drifting in and out of consciousness, and most of what he says isn't lucid."

"But he'll recover, won't he?" Emma asked. "That's what you're saying, isn't it?"

"That is what the doctor was insistent that we understand, my dear. Stuart's condition is extremely precarious."

Emma struggled to understand. W.C. Blythe's words sounded as if they were coming through a tunnel. "I'm not following you."

"What I'm trying to say, Emma, is that Stuart may not survive the night. Or even the next hour. His injuries are beyond what his body may be able to endure."

Emma's body shook with silent sobs.

"I can't tell you how sorry I am." The Wing Commander cleared his throat and took a moment to compose himself before continuing. "I haven't yet had the opportunity to congratulate you on your engagement. Stuart is a fine lad and--" he shook his head, unable to continue.

"Allow me a brief word with Will and Joanna," Andrej said as he strode to the doorway. "I'll take you to the hospital, Emma. Let me just sort out the children."

"I'm not certain that's a good idea." W.C. Blythe held out a hand to stop him. "Perhaps it would be better to wait until morning when I can update you on his condition."

Emma shot Andrej a pleading look.

He nodded. "We will go now."

THE DRIVE TO THE HOSPITAL SEEMED ENDLESS. EMMA GLANCED AT Andrej as he swung Will's Vauxhall into the car park. He hadn't spoken during the drive but his worried expression spoke volumes.

"I'm frightened."

Andrej nodded, turned the ignition off, and slipped the key into his jacket pocket. "I know you are. But I'll be there with you."

Emma squeezed her eyes shut, but there was no escape from the regret that consumed her. This was her fault. Even though the circumstances of Stuart's accident were as yet uncertain, she knew that it led back to her. Whether it was her fear, her lies, or her enemy who made this happen, it was her fault. She'd never hated herself more. "My God, Andrej, what have I done?"

He placed his hand gently over hers. "It's not what you've done that you should be thinking about, but what you can do now to help Stuart."

She nodded. "You're right, I'm sorry."

"Don't be sorry. None of this is your fault."

She tried to laugh off his misplaced faith in her but the sound came out as a choked sob instead. "Every decision I make seems to be completely wrong. All I want is to keep everyone around me safe, yet people are being threatened and hurt. I never meant for anything like this to happen."

Andrej got out of the car and came around to open her door. He helped her out and looked down at her. "You're fighting a battle against Malcolm for noble reasons, Emma. People get hurt in any conflict. But you owe it to Stuart now, and always to Patrick, to keep your wits about you and to fight as hard as you have to."

Emma looked up into Andrej's eyes, already knowing what she would find there. Warmth, compassion, kindness. And support. Support she was desperately grateful for.

She nodded. "Let's go see Stuart."

Andrej took her hand and slipped it through the crook of his arm just as he had the first night they met in London. Tonight there were no Nazi aircraft overhead or threats of falling bombs, but Emma felt even more frightened than she had then.

ANDREJ AND EMMA APPROACHED STUART'S BED SLOWLY, CAUTIONED BY the ward sister on duty that he was drifting in and out of consciousness.

"Your fiancé is in very grave condition, Miss Bradley," the night sister said as she straightened his pillow. Her motions, despite being gentle, elicited a moan from Stuart.

Andrej didn't miss the way Emma flinched at the sound.

Stuart lay heavily bandaged, his face almost completely covered in white gauze. His hands were bandaged as well but Andrej saw Stuart's blackened fingertips. A wave of nausea rolled over him. The young airman, who always spoke with warmth and sincerity, and moved with the energy of youth, now lay virtually lifeless before them. Only his shallow breathing and an occasional moan told of the life still within him.

Emma stepped closer to the bed and gingerly reached out to touch Stuart's shoulder. "Stuart, it's me, Emma. I'm here now," she whispered.

Andrej brought a chair to the bedside and gently guided Emma to sit. His hand lingered on her shoulder for a second before he drew back into the shadow. He felt powerless to do anything about the anguish he heard in her voice.

"Andrej's here too," Emma continued. "Stuart, I'm so sorry." She glanced back over her shoulder at Andrej. He nodded his encouragement.

"I'm here for you now." Her voice cracked, and she took a moment to compose herself before continuing. "Please hold on, Stuart. The doctors here are going to help you grow strong again."

Only silence answered Emma's pleas. She leaned over to rest her head near Stuart's shoulder. Her own shoulders shook with sobs.

They stayed at his bedside through the night. A clock dispassionately ticked away minute after minute, as Stuart's labored breathing struggled to keep up with the passing hours.

Andrej glanced down at Emma's head resting on his shoulder. From her breathing, he guessed she was finally asleep. She'd resisted his numerous attempts to take her back to the cottage for a few hours rest. Her stubborn refusal hadn't surprised him. Emma's loyalties ran deep and strong. He loved that about her.

His gaze traveled to Stuart. The lad had occasionally shifted, each movement followed by a low agonized moan. He hadn't regained consciousness though. Not once had he responded to Emma's voice.

A discreet cough came from the other side of the curtain.

"Andrej." The voice was just above a whisper.

Funny, it sounded like Will. Andrej slowly eased away from a sleeping Emma. As quietly as possible, he pulled the privacy curtain aside. It was Will, and he wore a grave expression.

"Come this way," Andrej led Will out into a corridor where they could speak privately. "Are the children all safe?"

Will nodded. "No worries on that account. Joanna and I have taken your warnings to heart. I'll be heading straight back myself in a moment." He took off his cap and twisted it in his hands. "How's the young lad?"

Andrej shook his head.

Will grimaced. "I'm sorry."

"Why are you here so early, Will?"

The older man looked at him, concern etched on his face. "Two policemen were at the cottage last night."

Andrej leaned against the wall, grateful for the support. This had to be about the letters. He knew the police would have questioned the German POW and have learned of their existence by now. Damnation. "What did they have to say?"

Will shifted from one foot to the other instead of answering the question. Andrej had never seen him look so uncomfortable.

"Was it in regards to Stuart's accident?" he asked.

"No, that's the part of it that is deuced awkward." Will glanced back to where Emma slept. "Their questions concerned Emma."

"What sort of questions?" Andrej tried to quell his mounting impatience. No, not impatience. Dread.

"They asked what we knew about her, how long she's been living with us, what we think of her. Questions like that."

"What did you tell them?"

Will looked surprised at the question. "We told them that she's a lovely young lady who works hard and takes wonderful care of the children. We told them she was the sort of girl anyone would be proud to have as a daughter."

Andrej nodded. "Did they ask any questions more specific than that?"

"They asked about the work you two did together, of which we know very little of course. And there were questions about her engagement to young Tollison." Will hesitated for a long moment. "We couldn't answer anything about that because it caught us off guard. Joanna and I thought that you and Emma...well, it seemed obvious to us that you two cared for each other."

"I'm sorry. I can't explain it now, but in due time, I will." Andrej glanced over his shoulder in the direction of Stuart's room. "Did they say they wished to speak with Emma?"

"Yes. They know she's here with Stuart." Will turned to leave but stopped. "I should tell you they searched her room."

An unspoken question hung between them.

"Will, listen carefully. Emma hasn't done anything wrong. I promise you that she's guilty of nothing except trying to keep Patrick safe from someone who wishes him harm. I want you and Joanna to understand that, to believe that."

Will held up his hand. "Say no more. Your word is good enough for us. I'd best get back to the cottage and the children. Just tell me that the lad is going to recover."

The truth stuck in Andrej's throat. He couldn't conjure up the lie they both wanted to hear.

"I'm sorry," Will finally managed. "What can we do for Emma?"

"Keep Patrick safe."

EMMA LIFTED HER HEAD WHEN SHE HEARD ANDREJ PULL ASIDE THE curtain.

"I'm sorry if I woke you," he said.

She shook her head. "You didn't. An orderly was just in to draw back the blackout curtains." She rubbed her eyes, stood and stretched. "I thought perhaps you'd gone home."

"I wouldn't leave you."

Tears welled in Emma's eyes. The tenderness in his voice was almost too much to bear. "Were you speaking with Stuart's doctor?"

"No, that was Will."

Something in the way Andrej wouldn't meet her gaze alarmed her. "Are the children safe?"

"Yes, Emma." Andrej crossed the room and stopped in front of her. He reached down and tucked a fallen wisp of her hair behind her ear. "Trust me when I say that Will and Joanna fully understand how important it is to keep the children safely inside the cottage."

"Thank goodness." She closed her eyes. She couldn't take any more worry just now. Her heart ached. Not once since they'd arrived had Stuart responded to her voice. Several times his eyes had fluttered open but just as quickly they closed again and he was lost to them.

The ward sister had explained that the amount of pain medication he was being given made it difficult for him to be lucid.

"Please consider the ward sister's offer of a bed, Emma. Just long enough to rest a bit."

"I don't want Stuart to be alone."

"He's unaware of time, my dear. I will stay here with him and I'll fetch you straight away when he wakes."

Emma shook her head. There was sense in what Andrej wanted her to do but she couldn't leave Stuart, not until she saw a sign, however slim, that he would recover. She'd been selfish enough already.

"Did Will bring news from W.C. Blythe about the accident?"

"No."

Emma glanced back at Andrej quickly. His terse tone surprised her. "You don't think it was an accident either, do you?"

Andrej's silence was answer enough.

A low moan came from Stuart's bed. "Emma." It sounded more like a croak than a spoken word but Emma could have cried for joy at the sound of it.

"Yes, Stuart, it's me." She wished she could touch his hand to reassure him that he wasn't alone but she doubted he'd be able to bear the pain. "I'm right here and I won't leave you."

"Water."

While Andrej helped elevate Stuart's pillow, Emma managed to get a small amount of water into his mouth. He closed his eyes again as Andrej gently lowered his head.

"Stuart, tell me what I can do for you," Emma pleaded. She would do anything, give anything, to ease his pain.

His eyelids fluttered open again. "Your uncle…you have to stay away…he was by the plane…."

Her uncle? The plane? He wasn't making any sense. It had to be the pain medication talking. She glanced up at Andrej for guidance.

"Stuart, who is Emma's uncle?" Andrej leaned over the bed rail, his voice low and urgent. "Come now, I know it's hard but I need you to tell me who you saw by your plane."

Stuart's eyes fluttered closed. Andrej's voice grew more insistent. "Stay with me, lad. I need your help. Focus on what I'm saying. Who did you see by the plane?"

The next words out of Stuart's mouth were incoherent.

Andrej tried again. "Help me to help Emma, please. You recognized who it was, didn't you?"

Emma had had enough. "No more questions. You've got to let him sleep, Andrej. He's fighting just to hold on."

"Malcolm." Stuart's voice wasn't strong but it was clear enough that they both heard him.

Emma felt the room start to spin. Why was he saying that Malcolm was her uncle? She clutched onto the bed frame and tried to steady herself.

"Tell me something more, son," Andrej urged Stuart. "You called him Emma's uncle. You knew this man?" Stuart's eyelids fluttered shut but Andrej persisted. "He told you he was Emma's uncle? Is that right, Stuart?"

Another groan. Emma's heart ached more with each passing moment. Stuart sounded as if he were in unbearable agony.

Stuart struggled but he was able to continue speaking. "Emma's uncle...Malcolm wanted to surprise her...always asked about the baby...."

Emma and Andrej waited but Stuart's next words were incomprehensible, eventually petering out until he was unconscious again.

Andrej leaned back in his chair and ran his fingers through his hair. "Good God, Emma, Malcolm did this." He looked straight at her, his eyes searching hers for confirmation she agreed.

She nodded dumbly. She was powerless to speak against the shock, disgust, and remorse that raged inside of her. She glanced at Stuart and began to cry again, not tears born of fear, but wracking sobs of shame and guilt.

Andrej came around the bed and gathered her into his arms. He whispered soothing words in Dutch, words she couldn't understand, but that nevertheless quieted her cries. He gently stroked her hair, his arms tight around her.

"Not now, my love. Time later for this, now you must be strong." He tilted her chin up and brushed a tender kiss across her forehead.

Emma sagged against him, not too proud to draw from his strength. She had none of her own left.

"I am going to leave you here with Stuart."

These were the last words she wanted to hear. "Where are you going?"

"To retrieve the letters in your room."

"I don't care about that now, Andrej. That can wait."

"No." He motioned his head toward Stuart lying nearly lifeless in the bed. "You can't believe this is the end of it. I'm afraid it's only just begun."

Andrej rested his hand on Stuart's heavily bandaged arm for a brief moment. "Fight on, son. We will be here to help you."

Emma watched as the curtain closed behind him. She covered her face with both hands to keep from crying out after him. From a seemingly endless reservoir of grief, more tears flowed.

"Emma." Stuart's speech sounded suddenly lucid, she clearly recognized her name.

"I'm right here, Stuart. Do you want me to find a doctor or the ward sister? Tell me what I can do to help you."

He took several deep, labored breaths before he spoke again. "Tell me about our life together." The six words seemed to spend what strength he had.

As if providence whispered it to her, Emma knew that her response needed to comfort Stuart for whatever time he had left. "The war can't last much longer, maybe only a few more months," she began. "After that we go wherever you wish." She swallowed the lump in her throat and fought to keep her voice level. "We can go north to the Lake District to be near your family. After a few years, we can buy a small cottage, would you like that?"

"If you were there." His voice had a lightness, a tranquility, that hadn't been there just moments before.

Emma forged ahead, desperate to say anything that would comfort him. "We can plant flowers in the spring. I know you're keen on gardening. You can teach me, I would love a garden full of roses. We'll have Patrick, and perhaps we'll be blessed with more children--"

"A little girl with curls."

Emma's breath caught. Stuart's voice was strong, as if by some miracle he had shed the pain that cursed him. He turned his head and his eyes locked onto hers.

"Yes, that would be lovely." She remembered the way Stuart teased her about her unruly curls. He'd never seen her hair down. She reached up and pulled her hairpins out. Her hair tumbled about her shoulders. Her heart began to race when he lifted a hand to touch one of her curls.

"Stuart, thank you." She gingerly took his hand in hers. He didn't flinch when she touched him. "Thank you for being so kind to me, for wanting to help me, and for being my friend. Most especially, for wanting to be my husband." She bit back fresh tears when he gently squeezed her hand.

How was he moving through the pain? She thought of the few true friends she'd had in her life. He was among them. There was so much more she needed to say. "I love you, Stuart."

A gentle sigh preceded his last breath. As Emma felt the strength leave his hand, she knew it was too late for anyone or anything to ever hurt him again. She lowered her head against Stuart's chest and, through quiet tears, offered a silent prayer of gratitude for the brief but kind life he'd lived.

She had no idea how long it was before the ward sister came and touched her on the shoulder. "I'm so sorry, Miss Bradley."

Emma lifted her head and gazed at the nurse as if through a haze.

"Come with me, my dear."

Emma allowed herself to be led down a corridor. Her heart and mind both numb, she settled onto a bench and waited as she was bid while the nurse went in search of a doctor.

Moments later an orderly stood in front of her.

"Miss Bradley?"

She nodded, grief leaving her unable to speak.

The young man handed her a folded note. "A messenger has just brought this for you."

Emma reached for the paper. She waited until the orderly left before she opened the note. She blinked several times until she could see through her tears.

Slowly, the words morphed into a sickening shape.

My Dear Emma,

Forgive my belated response to the news of your engagement. Please accept my heartfelt wishes for a lifetime of happiness for you and your husband-to-be.

Your devoted servant,

Malcolm

CHAPTER 17

*E*mma's back ached. She gingerly shifted on the wooden bench, trying not to wake Patrick as she did so. He'd become increasingly fussy. Accustomed to being nursed, he'd refused the bottle she'd offered. Finally, worn out from screaming, he'd fallen into a fitful sleep.

A passing porter assured her that the train she was waiting for would soon be along. She forced herself to smile until he'd moved past her, but it hurt too much to keep up the façade that all was well. Tears pricked at the back of her eyes. It was hard to believe that her body could produce yet more tears. She'd gone through a lifetime's worth since she'd learned of Stuart's accident the night before. The memory of his ready smile and easy manner pulled at her heart. She would never forget him, or the fact he died because Malcolm wanted to frighten her into giving him the damning evidence she had against him.

She was as much to blame for Stuart's death as Malcolm was. How could she have been so unbearably stupid to think she could hold on to proof of Malcolm's treason without there being a question of her complicity?

She closed her eyes and took a deep breath. She needed to focus on the only thing that really mattered. Patrick. Until he was safely out of harm's way she couldn't make Malcolm pay for the lives he'd taken. She pulled the blanket over the baby's head as he snuggled into her shoulder.

Emma stood and hitched her one small bag up on her shoulder when her train's arrival was announced.

"Here's your train, Miss." A porter she'd spoken with earlier stopped beside her and looked about for her case.

"I don't have any luggage," she answered his unspoken question.

"You must be heading home then." His smile was wide. "Have a pleasant journey, Miss." With a quick touch to the brim of his hat, he was gone.

Home. The word reverberated through Emma's mind, forcing her to question her choice to run away. She watched the newly arrived passengers stream onto the platform. Most walked with certainty, as if they knew where they were and where they were going. She watched them; young and old, couples, families, and single people purposefully striding somewhere. Home. They were heading home, to their families, and friends. To their safe place in the world where they belonged.

"Oh, Cora, look at the wee babe." A pair of elderly ladies stopped in front of Emma. They both wore broad smiles. The taller of the two leaned in to see Patrick's face. "What a little cherub he is, sleeping like that."

The one named Cora put her hand over her heart. "My goodness but you're a fortunate young woman to have such a beautiful baby." Her eyes grew dreamy. "And the time goes by so swiftly, don't you know. I was about your age when I had my little Jimmy, the first of four. Mind you, he's a grandfather himself now."

"Yes, it does go by quickly," her friend mused. She straightened and smiled, her eyes kind. "Well, we mustn't keep you, my dear. I imagine you're on your way home now."

Home? No. She was running away. Running away from Malcolm and his threats, and thereby ensuring that her son would never have a normal life.

After she'd exchanged a moment more of pleasantries with the two strangers, she heard her boarding announcement. She should move, get on the train, go back to London so that she could...what? Make a new plan to hide elsewhere? Enjoy a brief respite before Malcolm tracked them down again? She glanced down at Patrick. He was so tiny, so unaware. For now. But for how long could she hide her fear of Malcolm from him? How long would they be on the run? Malcolm killed Patricia. He was responsible for Stuart's death. Who next? She tightened her hold on Patrick. This had to stop. *She* had to stop. She was done running.

She dropped a kiss on her son's head. "Let's go home, sweetheart." Home to sweet little Lily, home to mischievous but loveable Peter, and home to Andrej. She owed him an apology. She'd wronged him by not giving him the trust he deserved. But she was ready to right that wrong. Whatever they faced in stopping Malcolm, they'd face it together. And after that, she'd do everything she could to convince him that she and Patrick wanted him. Needed him. She quickened her steps.

~

"You have the letters?"

"Yes, for the hundredth time, Lily. They're in a safe place." Peter immediately regretted snapping at his sister but his nerves were on edge enough without her constant questions.

"You needn't be so ugly about it."

"I know," he conceded. "I'm sorry. The adults are all behaving strangely and no one will answer my questions. It's driving me mad."

They sat at the top of the stairs in silence. Every few minutes one of the grown-ups would poke their head around the corner to ensure they were still in sight. Twice they had asked to go out and play but Uncle Will had turned them down both times without an explanation. Aunt Joanna and Mrs. Morrison were acting just as peculiarly.

"I wish I knew where Aunt Emma went," Lily finally said.

"Well, we'll never know if no one around here will talk to us." Peter sighed. "I wish I knew why Mr. Van der Hoosen left in such a hurry."

Lily shrugged. "At least he didn't catch you stealing the letters from Aunt Emma. That's a good thing."

That it was. He and Lily were in complete agreement that whatever trouble Aunt Emma was in, it centered around the packet of letters hidden in her room. Therefore, they reasoned, getting rid of the letters would make Aunt Emma's problems disappear. Fortunately, they'd been able to get to the letters before the police had come round.

"I still can't believe that Flight Lieutenant Tollison has died," Lily said.

Peter nodded. He felt sad. And guilty.

"We weren't very kind to him," Lily mused.

"I know." Peter sighed. "He wasn't a bad chap. He just got in the way of Aunt Emma and Mr. Van der Hoosen."

Lily sighed. "We obviously didn't get them to fall in love, did we?"

Peter didn't bother to respond. Adults were beyond control. Beyond understanding even.

"Now tell me what we're going to do with the letters?" Lily turned to him, wearing a worried frown. "Which adult should we give them to?"

"Give them to an adult?" he scoffed. "I hardly think that's the answer."

"Then what are you going to do with them?"

"I've already done it. I've buried them where no one will ever find them," Peter said. "And now they're gone, Aunt Emma's problems will be over once and for all."

ANDREJ FELT AS IF HIS HEAD WAS GOING TO EXPLODE, OR MAYBE IT WAS his heart. Either way, he was well along the road to madness without knowing where Emma and Patrick were. They'd only been gone a matter of hours, yet it already felt like a lifetime.

He paced the rail station platform as if it were a cage. He still wasn't certain that leaving Brighton in search of Emma was a wise move but he couldn't wait any longer for something to happen. More to the point, he was unwilling to sit and wait for Malcolm to make his next move. It took every ounce of self-control he had to not find Malcolm and end his miserable life.

The only solution was to find Emma first and convince her they should deal with Malcolm together. She wasn't going to be happy when she learned he'd left the children, but Will, Joanna and Iris had vowed not to let their guard down in his absence.

A glance at his pocket watch informed him that he had only moments left to find Emma before the train departed. Andrej heard the announcement that the train for London was boarding. He crossed over to platform three and joined the queue. Although he didn't know where Emma was headed, she'd likely have to pass through London. However impossible it seemed, he would find a way to trail her from there. It was unlikely she would stay long in the city. The Blitz was turning London into a living nightmare. No, Emma would pass through as quickly as she could because her first priority would be to keep Patrick safe.

Andrej settled into a seat and tried to concentrate on reading a newspaper a previous passenger had left behind but it proved impossible. The only thing he could think of was finding Emma and Patrick and bringing them both home. He refolded the newspaper and laid it on the empty seat beside him.

He glanced out the window at those waiting on the platform. He shot to his feet when he caught sight of Emma, Patrick bundled in her arms, heading for the car park.

He turned toward the exit and cursed when he bumped into a ticket collector.

"Hear now, there's no call for that sort of language." He narrowed his eyes as he looked up at Andrej. "Say now, were you speaking German just now?"

"No." Andrej said as he moved to step past him but the other man didn't budge.

"You're German."

"I'm not." Andrej struggled to keep the frustration out of his voice. "I'm Dutch."

The other man eyed him appraisingly. "Be that as it may, you're still a foreigner." He studied Andrej's clothing and then leveled a doubtful stare at him. "You're awfully well dressed for a refugee."

"I'm not a refugee."

The ticket collector scowled. "You're saying there's something wrong with being a refugee?"

Good God, why now? "Let me pass, please."

He cocked his head to the side and studied Andrej. "You're in a frightful hurry, aren't you?"

When the final whistle blew and the 'all aboard' call went out, desperation drove Andrej to lie. "My wife and baby son are out there." He pointed through the window. "There's been a miscommunication and I need to catch up with them." Heaven knew that was the truth. And he would marry Emma the first chance he had. It was no longer about protecting her from Malcolm. It was about living every moment he had left with her and Patrick.

"Your wife you say? Was she wearing a red coat and holding a baby? I remember her." He gave a low whistle. "She's a lovely one, your wife, with those beautiful curls and quite a shapely--" He coughed, apparently deciding that no further description was necessary. "Wait, she'd been crying. That's right. She sat on that bench over there and cried. The poor soul." He frowned. "What did you do to her?"

Andrej stifled a groan. This had to be a bad dream. "I'm sure that she was. She recently lost her--" he caught himself before he said fiancé.

"You didn't hurt her?"

"I swear on your King's life I would never hurt her." Those words were the truest he'd ever spoken. "I need to find her to make sure she's safe. I want to take her home, back to the people who love her." The train gave a lurch forward.

The ticket collector shook his head. "Why are you standing around here chatting with me then?" He stood aside. "Go on. Find your wife."

Andrej called his thanks over his shoulder as he ran to the vestibule. He pulled back the lever, slid the door open, and leapt to the platform.

∼

"ARE YOU SURE YOU REMEMBER YOUR INSTRUCTIONS?" PETER ASKED THE man who crouched behind the sofa. "I can go over everything again if need be."

The man rolled his eyes. "Instead of worrying about my memory, you'd best be worrying about my legs going numb and your criminal getting away before I can stand up properly."

Lily leaned over the sofa and frowned at him. "He's not our criminal, Sir. He's meant to be yours. If you'll just cooperate for a little while longer you'll be able to catch a murderer."

"Murder is very serious business, young lady, and not an allegation that I can take lightly."

"You don't believe us?" Lily demanded. "After everything we've told you about this man?"

"I never said I didn't believe you. But you must understand that I can't accuse someone of murder just on your say so."

"But if you overhear a confession then you can take him to jail, can't you?" Lily looked at her brother, her eyes wide. "Isn't that what you said, Peter?"

"Yes, Lily, that is exactly what is going to happen. Isn't it, Constable Barnes?"

"If it isn't, my sister will have my head on a platter."

"I know all about scary sisters." Peter winked at Lily.

"That's quite enough out of you two," Iris scolded them. "I still think this idea is sheer lunacy."

"Do you have a better one?" Peter asked.

Iris frowned at him. "Don't be cheeky, young man."

"I didn't mean to be, Mrs. Morrison. Honestly. But everything I told you about this man is the God's truth." He turned to his sister. "Isn't it, Lily?"

She nodded somberly. "We heard it directly from Aunt Emma's mouth. Mr. Van der Hoosen believed her. I think we should as well."

"Don't get too smug, young man," Iris' brother advised Peter. "This Malcolm character doesn't sound like he's stupid, so be careful not to tip him off. You'd do much better to act afraid and let him think he has the upper hand. He should be here shortly. Iris, go into the kitchen and keep that iron skillet at the ready."

Iris nodded. "I'd love the chance to cosh him over the head with it." She gave her brother a pointed look. "Keep these children safe or your skull will be the one what gets coshed."

A sharp knock at the front door arrested the words Peter was about to say. He swallowed hard.

"Wait here for him to come in," Constable Barnes whispered, his voice suddenly sharp. "Stay right here on the sofa where I can grab you if necessary. Do you understand?"

Both children nodded their agreement while Iris dashed into the kitchen.

"Now call for him to come in."

Peter did as instructed. He held his breath. A moment later, the front door creaked open.

"We're in the sitting room," he called out again.

"Come out here," Malcolm ordered them.

"Sorry, we can't," Lily took a turn shouting out. "We told the adults that we wouldn't move off the sofa until they came home."

Silence. Peter glanced at Lily. Her lower lip was trembling. In some crazy way, her fear made him feel braver.

"Your letters are in here," Peter said, loudly enough so that his voice would carry. He reached over and squeezed Lily's hand.

MALCOLM PUSHED OPEN THE SITTING ROOM DOOR CAUTIOUSLY. THE fact that no one had come to the door to answer his knock was suspicious. Hell, the fact that he was here at this blasted hovel at all was downright ludicrous. But the children had mentioned the letters when he'd rung to speak with Emma. That was reason enough to come.

The two brats were sitting on the sofa, hand in hand.

"Where are the adults who are supposed to be watching you?" he asked. "Call them in here."

"Say please."

A command from a little girl? He balled his fists.

"I've come for the letters you mentioned when I phoned." His gaze swept the room. Not a single letter was in sight. Something wasn't right. The children looked eager almost.

They were up to something.

The voice of reason warned him to leave but he couldn't resist one more attempt. "Give me the letters and I will go."

"What did the letters say?" It was the boy this time.

"Where's Emma?" Malcolm countered.

The children exchanged glances. Their reaction told him all that he needed to know. Rage shot through him. The lying bitch had set him up.

"Why did you kill Lieutenant Tollison?" the boy asked.

Malcolm narrowed his eyes. The only two places that someone could be hiding were either behind the door or behind the sofa. He walked slowly toward the door and leaned against it as casually as possible. It flattened against the wall. No one was there. Surely Emma was not stupid enough to think she could use the children to trick him into a confession?

"I'm sorry, lad. I have no idea who or what you are referring to." He took a step toward them but the little girl let out a shriek that stopped him cold.

"Stay back," she cried. "You're a murderer. A Nazi-loving murderer."

"Shut up." Malcolm felt the familiar tremor in his body, the feeling he always got just before he hurt someone. He struggled to hold his temper in check. There had to be an adult around. The children wouldn't have been left alone. He should leave before he lost what precious little self-control he still had.

"I don't understand why you had to kill Lieutenant Tollison when it's Aunt Emma that you hate."

The boy was playing with fire. Taunting him.

"We do have the letters you know," the girl said. "We'll give them to you too. But first you have to promise you won't hurt Aunt Emma or Patrick the way you hurt Stuart. Or the way you hurt Patrick's mother."

He couldn't hold his tongue any longer. "Patrick's mother was a pathetic whore--"

"Shut up, Malcolm."

He whirled around. Hatred coursed through him at the sight of Emma. She was all that was wrong with his life. She was the threat that dogged his every move, the worry that kept him awake at night. No one else had a clue what alliances he'd made. No one else made a connection between him and that ridiculous woman who got herself pregnant with his bastard. Silencing Patricia was supposed to have brought him peace.

Until, that was, Emma had vowed revenge and denied him the quiet he deserved. She'd stolen the letters from his office while he was attending Patricia's funeral. Her taunting threats still rang in his ears. She would be the one to set the hounds of hell after him for that useless lieutenant's death.

"You won't get away with it, Malcolm." Emma stepped closer to him.

Damn her, why wasn't she afraid of him? She should be. He could so easily slide his hands around her throat and make the noise stop. He could silence her. His palms itched.

"I won't let you get away with killing Stuart the way you got away with murdering Patricia." She came closer still. Her eyes were fixed on his, furious, unblinking. The sparks of rage he saw there mesmerized him. He understood the rage, his own was driving him now. Compelling him to silence her. For good.

"Why did you do it, Malcolm?" Her voice sounded as if it were coming through a dark tunnel, straight for him. It wouldn't stop. Her voice, her questions, were relentless, unyielding, demanding…he wanted it to stop. He had to make it stop.

"Just tell me, why did you kill Stuart? Say it." She was baiting him. She came closer. Her voice was growing louder. "You're a coward to kill him and not be able to say it. Say it."

In a blinding fury driven rage Malcolm lunged for her throat. As he wrapped his fingers around her neck a thrill went through him, intensifying as he tightened his grip. Voices he couldn't separate filled his head. Screaming…it had to be the children. He pressed his thumbs harder into Emma's flesh, spurred on by her gurgling gasps for air.

Euphoria was making him light headed. He heard another voice, this one gloating about petrol, a cigarette match and a Spitfire. Fuel. Flames.

And then there was darkness. And silence.

CHAPTER 18

When Emma stepped back into Laurel Cottage the next morning, she braced herself as Peter and Lily flew down the stairs and straight into her arms.

"Careful now," Will warned them. "Emma's been through an ordeal."

Ordeal. That was one way to describe having Malcolm's hands round her neck, his thumbs pressing so hard that she'd had to fight to breathe.

Joanna appeared in the hallway, a broad smile on her face. After the children released Emma, she took a turn and hugged Emma tight. "Thank heavens you're home, my dear. We've been sick with worry."

Emma smiled weakly. "You cannot imagine how good it feels to be here."

"Come this way, there's a certain young man anxious to see his mum," Iris hailed Emma from the kitchen.

Emma allowed the children to lead her there, touched by their solicitous manner. She gratefully sank into the chair Will pulled out for her. She reached out for Patrick. "Hello, my sweet baby," she cooed as she held him up in front of her. "How is my precious boy?" When his face broke into a smile of recognition, she gave a half-sob and half-laugh. "I missed you, darling boy."

Iris placed a steaming cup of tea in front of Emma. She pulled a chair next to her and smiled. "Go on then, love, have a nice long drink and then start talking." She grinned. "Now that we know you're home to stay we want to hear everything." A shadow of concern flashed across her face. "You are here to stay, aren't you?"

Emma shifted the baby to the crook of her arm and tightened her hold on him possessively. "For now." Her free hand went to her throat, still sore from Malcolm's attempt to strangle her.

Iris leaned over and gently moved Emma's hand away. She gasped. "My God, that man is a monster. I'm so sorry that he did this to you."

"Don't be. If Malcolm hadn't attacked me then he wouldn't be in police custody. I owe my life to your brother. When he flew over the sofa and pulled Malcolm off of me, he was an angel."

Iris squeezed her hand. "What you ought to thank him for is not letting Andrej kill Malcolm. When he burst through the door and saw what Malcolm was doing to you, he looked ready to snap Malcolm's neck." She shuddered. "We'd have had the wrong man swinging from the end of a noose if that had happened."

Will coughed and gave a pointed look at a wide-eyed Peter and Lily. Emma winced. Her priority now should be helping the children recover from what they'd seen.

"Peter and Lily, I am so sorry for what you witnessed," she said, feeling her words to be totally inadequate. "You must have been terribly frightened."

Peter gave a shrug that was meant to be nonchalant. "It was all part of the plan."

"Oh, honestly, Peter." Lily shot him an exasperated look before turning to Emma. "Did the police come visit you while you were in hospital?"

Emma nodded. "There were dozens of questions to answer, along with paperwork and interviews. It was late when they left."

"It was early enough when they were around here this morning,"

Will said. He glanced up at the clock. "Andrej must still be in conference with the Detective Chief Superintendent."

How she would ever be able to thank Andrej for the way he'd advocated for her with the police last night? He'd been forceful, yet diplomatic, in the way he'd helped them see that she was one of Malcolm's victims, and not his accomplice. "That's quite a tale about you leading the police to the letters, Peter."

He swallowed hard. "You heard about that, did you?"

"I did," Emma assured him. The letters. In the beginning, when she'd first decided to steal them from Malcolm, they'd seemed the perfect insurance to keep Malcolm from trying to take Patrick from her. But as time went on, the fact she was holding on to potentially treasonous information, she began to think they would be her undoing.

But when Andrej had left her hospital room the night Stuart had died, he'd assured her that he would find a way to turn her possession of them into something that would help, and not hurt, her. After, of course, they were located. "Do you want to explain what happened this morning when the police came around?"

"Not especially, no," Peter answered.

Lily elbowed him.

"We buried them," Peter admitted.

"We?" Lily demanded.

Peter frowned at her. "It's been us from the start, Lily. No outs now."

"Fine." She turned to Emma. "We buried them."

"Why on earth would you do that?" Iris demanded.

"At least we didn't flush them down the loo," Peter said. "This way, we were able to show the police where they were." He looked between the adults. "And they were none the worse for wear, mind you. I wrapped them in brown paper."

Out of the corner of her eye, Emma saw that both Will and Joanna were struggling to retain their composure in the face of Peter's self-defense. She glanced at Iris, who sat looking at the ceiling. Clearly, they weren't meant to be of much help. She turned her attention back to the children. "Why did you bury them?"

"We decided that the letters were causing your troubles and it would be better if you were rid of them," Peter said, his voice sheepish.

"Did it occur to either of you that perhaps disposing of the letters might have made things worse for Emma?" Will asked.

The children nodded gravely.

"We thought of that," Lily said.

"After we'd buried them," Peter added. "It was too late by then to ask anyone."

Emma hardly knew what to say. While the children had no right to dispose of her property, she knew their intentions had been pure. The letters were now safely in possession of the authorities. In truth, Peter and Lily's actions hadn't done any damage.

Joanna pushed herself to her feet. "Let us not forget there's school to get ready for."

Peter's eyes widened. "Surely not today?"

Joanna's raised eyebrow answered his question without the need for words. Both children hugged Emma in turn before dashing upstairs to ready themselves for the day ahead.

When Will and Joanna made to follow them, Emma asked them to wait. She owed them an apology as well. "I'm sorry," she began, "I know my actions have brought chaos and violence in to your home. I hardly know how to apologize properly."

The Metcalfs exchanged a look. "You needn't apologize, my dear girl," Will said. "We understand that you've been frightened all along. We were parents too, remember." He took his wife's hand in his. "It's only natural that you'd do anything you had to do to protect your son. We'd have done no less."

Humbled by their graciousness, Emma had to force herself to speak. "I lied to you both on many occasions."

Joanna nodded. "We knew early on that things weren't just so. The first day you were here, I noticed that your ration booklet wasn't the proper color. I'll confess that worried me, but we've come to love you and Patrick, and Peter and Lily, as if you're our own family."

Will grinned. "It's taken a horrible war to bring us all together but I appreciate a houseful after so many years of quiet. Now, enough of this talk. It's over, and we've the children to sort out now." He glanced upwards. The children could be heard tromping around upstairs. "Peter's a fine lad, but he bears watching."

Iris gave a wry smile as the couple made their way from the room. "Therein might be the greatest understatement of 1940." Her expression grew serious. "I suppose it's my turn to apologize now, isn't it?" she said. Without waiting for Emma to agree, she forged ahead. "You have every right to be angry with me for agreeing with Peter's plan to trap Malcolm." Iris rolled her eyes heavenward. "I don't know what possessed me to even listen to Peter's plan, let alone participate. I mean, it wasn't as if you hadn't warned me what a horribly vile creature Malcolm was--"

"Iris--" Emma tried to interject, to no avail.

"--I most assuredly did know, but I also knew we couldn't leave you and Patrick defenseless. We had to help. Not that I think for a moment that I should have involved the children but--"

"Iris, please--" Emma tried again but her friend sailed ahead like a steamship powering through still waters.

"--my brother agreed, and you've seen how big he is. I trusted him when he assured me that he could keep the children safe. But then you burst in the room, your eyes were blazing, and for a moment I feared--"

Emma reached out and pinched Iris' arm.

"Oww, what was that for?"

"It seemed the only way to stop you," Emma answered. "You don't need to apologize. The fault is entirely mine for not being here with Peter and Lily. I should have been, but instead I ran away. I'm ashamed of how cowardly I acted."

Iris reached for her hand and gave it a gentle squeeze. "You were trying to protect your son, Emma. There isn't a mother in England who wouldn't have done the same." She smiled brightly. "The important thing is that you came back just in time to drive Malcolm into such a fury that he confessed. That part worked out brilliantly."

Emma didn't know if brilliant was the word she would have chosen but she appreciated her friend's support. "Have Will and Joanna forgiven you for sending them away from the cottage on a fool's errand when all this was going on?"

Iris shrugged. "They don't appear to be overly upset. I think they're just terribly relieved it's all over." She thought a moment. "It is over, isn't it?"

Emma blew out a long breath as she shifted Patrick to her shoulder. She took a moment to consider her answer. "I don't know," she finally said. "You and your brother can vouch for Malcolm's confession to killing both Patricia and Stuart." Her voice broke when she said their names. She doubted a day would ever come when it wouldn't hurt to think of them. "So that alone should send Malcolm to the gallows."

"What about the letters?" Iris asked. "Surely they're proof of treason?"

"I hope not," Emma answered. "I'd have a lot to answer for in that case because I had them in my possession. Andrej read through them and didn't believe their content was sufficiently incriminating. We'll have to see if the D.C.S. agrees after he has them translated."

"I rather wish Peter had flushed them down the loo." Iris stood. "I'd best get home and rescue my brother from my children."

They were halfway down the hall when the front door opened and Andrej filled the doorway. His eyes locked with Emma's.

Her breath caught in her throat. The sight of him reassured her, delighted her, excited her, and most of all, made her feel whole.

"Well, then," Iris looked between them. "Why don't I just take Patrick home with me so you two can talk?"

"No." Andrej walked toward them. He reached out and took a sleepy Patrick into his arms. He brushed a gentle kiss across the baby's head and settled him onto his shoulder. "No, thank you, Iris. Patrick needs to be here for the discussion Emma and I are about to have."

A delighted grin stole over Iris' face as she looked between them.

"Does he, now? Well, I'll be off then." She turned around when she reached the door. "But I'll be back later." With a quick wink, she let herself out, leaving them facing each other.

Emma tried to speak but the words wouldn't come. Her eyes greedily drank in the sight of the two people she loved most in the world. The way Andrej gently swayed from side to side as he patted the baby's back told her all she needed to know. She loved this man. And she wanted him.

Forever.

"You're safe," Andrej said. "The D.C.S. doesn't feel the letters are proof of anything beyond Malcolm's questionable character. Seeing as there's no proof you tried to blackmail him, there's nothing he can charge you with."

"Malcolm won't face treason charges?"

Andrej shook his head. "But he'll stand trial for both murders."

Emma's throat was too thick with tears to easily respond. Nothing could bring her cousin or Stuart back, but at least Malcolm would pay with his life for taking theirs. "It's over," she finally managed to say.

Andrej reached out and caressed her cheek. "We need to talk about what's before us, not behind us."

Emma reached up and curled her fingers over his. It took everything she had to keep her breathing even the way her heart was racing. "What's before us?"

A smile stretched across his face. "You, me, our son."

"Our son," she repeated, her voice just above a whisper.

Andrej pulled her toward him and held her tight against him. "I love you, Emma. When I walked in here and saw Malcolm's choking you, I knew all that I wanted was to hold you close forever. Nothing else matters but the three of us. I've found my family in you two." He leaned down and brushed a kiss across her lips. "Marry me. Tomorrow, or as soon as I can procure a license."

Emma laughed. "Yes, if you're sure you know what you're--"

He silenced her with a kiss, one that left her with no doubt he knew exactly what he wanted.

EPILOGUE

October 19, 1942

Dear Uncle Andrej,

We received your last letter two days ago. The postman gave it to me to give to Aunt Emma and I wish you'd been here to see how happy she was when she heard that you'd written. After the mid-day meal, she read a bit of it to us; minus what the censors marked out and also, thankfully, the lovey-dovey mushy parts. Lily, the silly girl, still doesn't seem to grasp why you chose to join up and go off to fight but I do. I'd have done quite the same thing had I been in your shoes.

Everyone here at the cottage is well. Just as you asked of me, I help Uncle Will with anything I'm able to. Lily is still bossing me around and scolding me, so that should assure you she's her old self. Mum and Granny came down from London to visit us last week and stayed for four days. It was brilliant to see them. But, as you might imagine, there was a virtual flood of tears when it was time for them to catch their train home. My dad is still in a POW camp but Granny assures me that we should be grateful that he's at least accounted for, which I suppose is true. As I mentioned in my last letter, Laurel Manor is swarming with American GI's. They say the funniest things, and they can be awfully loud at times. Aunt Iris assures me that the more

Yanks that arrive, the sooner the war will be over with. I don't know if I believe that, but they're an amusing lot.

Aunt Emma is well. I know she misses you dreadfully. How can I be so certain? I'll tell you – each night after she's put Patrick and Willa to bed, she either sits and re-reads your letters or she writes to you. Patrick is toddling about now and he wants to put everything in his mouth. Rest assured, I watch him carefully. Baby Willa, well, I have to say that she's a good baby, for a girl, that is. When you see her next, you won't believe how much she's grown. As to when that might be, I wish we knew. I wish the war was over with, I wish that my dad would come home to England and we could go back to London. But, as Prime Minister Churchill says, we must soldier on, each one of us, until victory is ours.

Please stay safe. I assure you that I'm watching over your children as if they were my own brother and sister. I look forward to the day when I see you next. Until then, I remain respectfully yours,

Peter

Thank you for reading *A Love So True*. My hope is that you enjoyed reading it. I would be most grateful if you would consider leaving a review, however brief, wherever you purchased this e-book. Doing so helps other readers decide if this is a book they might enjoy, and it also lets me know if you'd like me to write more romances set in the World War II era.

~

I always enjoy hearing from readers, so please drop me a line via email at caroline@carolinemickelson.com or visit my website www.carolinemickelson.com to sign-up for my reader newsletter. I'd love to hear from you!

Printed by BoD˜in Norderstedt, Germany